HOME TO *Lanka*

A Novella in Five Movements

RAJ PAVAN

PARTRIDGE

A Penguin Random House Company

To order additional copies of this book, contact
Toll Free 800 101 2657 (Singapore)
Toll Free 1 800 81 7340 (Malaysia)
orders.singapore@partridgepublishing.com

www.partridgepublishing.com/singapore

"Home is the place where, when you have to go there,
They have to take you in."
"I should have called it
Something you somehow haven't to deserve."

—Robert Frost, "The Death of the Hired Man"

I

COLOMBO

Airports are maddening thresholds, compounded as they are of fear and anxiety, the severance of ties, however brief or long, and the tensions of the interregnum between the past and the future, a perfect rendition of the luminal structures of a life. Kumaran experienced all of these feelings as he stood in line at the Madras airport waiting to board the plane to Colombo. It was a long line, containing passengers clustered together rather unevenly and clutching odd assortments of bags and other packages. It was taking longer than it should as the clerk checked the tickets and weighed each box and suitcase. It seemed that everyone had excess baggage. They all argued and grumbled and, at times, cursed the clerk as they paid the fees.

Kumaran stood calmly enough, but he was impatient. He was keen to arrive in Colombo and see familiar faces and places. He had been living in London and New York for nearly three decades and had come home to Lanka only infrequently over the last few years. He knew that this return would be different, though. His father had died the year before and he had not been able to go to the funeral. There were other differences. He was older now, and at fifty-five, he was near the end of his own life—at least his professional life. Not perhaps at the end, but he was at a point where it was difficult to start anew anywhere. It was no longer possible, in fact, to return to Lanka with any prospect of work.

He turned around and looked at his fellow passengers as they settled in their seats. A young man sat next to him, perhaps in his early thirties, with dark wavy hair and a swarthy complexion. He had an alert and eager expression and the manner of someone who was quite sure of himself.

"I hope we leave on time," his neighbour said. "I am told that they are always late."

"Yes," Kumaran said. "Well, maybe today will be an exception. I have never seen such a mess as at this airport."

"You should see Heathrow—a mass of confusion."

"Are you a tourist?" Kumaran asked.

"No, I work in Sri Lanka. I'm a visiting professor at Peradeniya for a year. Do you live in Colombo?"

"No," Kumaran said, savouring the moment. "I live in New York. I work for the UN." The stewardess, whose plump and bounteous body was elegantly contained in a tightly wrapped saree, came down the aisle and checked the seat belts. Kumaran turned to his companion and asked, "What do you teach?"

"English, English as a second language." The man paused a moment. "I am from New York. I was brought up in Brooklyn. When were you last in Sri Lanka?"

"I was last here about two years ago, for a short visit."

"Surely you must have spent your home leave in Sri Lanka?" his neighbour asked, knowing that, every two years, the UN sends its employees home on leave for three months.

"No, I did not declare Lanka as my home when I joined the UN I'm now a US citizen. I do economic research, and it does not require field experience."

"I suppose the conditions in Sri Lanka aren't very inviting. It is all so terrible. It seems so unnecessary."

"Yes," Kumaran said. He looked away, unwilling to be drawn into a discussion on this topic. He noticed that he still referred to his island home as Lanka, while foreigners used the official name, Sri Lanka. Historically, the island was simply called Lanka and later Ceylon by the British, but then it was changed to Sri Lanka by politicians seeking to define it as glorious and blessed, a priori. The people did not acknowledge that prefix in their everyday parlance, though. Their country's name was simply "Lanka."

"I've been reading up on the conflicts in Sri Lanka, and I admit I can't make sense out of it."

"It is just another one of those conflicts between two groups of people who speak different languages and have different cultures that were forced together by the British," replied Kumaran. "They are finding it increasingly difficult to live together."

"What will happen now?"

"I don't know. That is the tragedy of the Tamils. They have to live amidst the Sinhalese, but the Sinhalese are not particularly fond of them. Kumaran then asked his neighbour, whose name it turned out was Aram, whether he had seen much of Lanka.

"Yes, indeed. I have been all over the west coast. The beaches are truly wonderful, and I have gone to Nuwara Eliya as well, and places upcountry."

"I have never been to Nuwara Eliya," Kumaran said. "Never had the time or occasion when I lived here. I may go up there this time."

They were interrupted by the stewardess who had arrived with the disembarkation forms.

"It is truly beautiful," Aram said. "The tea country is especially irresistible."

"Yes, I am planning to go there later in my visit."

As he filled out the forms, Kumaran found himself feeling troubled about home and abroad. He now had to include his American passport number and the visa number issued by the Lankan consulate in New York. He had to get a visa to enter his birthplace, his motherland, his homeland, and to claim his birthright.

His father had left him a small piece of land in his village in Jaffna, the northern province of the island, according to the traditional law of the region which insisted that all the property that a man inherited from his father should be transferred to his son. Kumaran had come all the way from America to claim this birthright and take possession of it. Of course, Kumaran could buy a bigger plot of land somewhere else, a bigger house in the metropolis, but ancestral property was a different matter altogether.

His brother, Shanmugam, had written to say that Kumaran should come and "do something" about the land. Kumaran thought about him. Shan had taken his own birthright with a house on it, expanded it, and decided to live his life on it. He had also taken the fertile land that was part of the family property and made it profitable. The family was a "respectable" land-owning family, and their father was known in the local parlance as a "landed proprietor," a verbal concoction made either by a British civil servant or a local one. His brother had decided to stay at home and cultivate the land, or to put it more accurately, have it cultivated by his tenants while he pursued his career as a lawyer.

Shanmugam did well in both enterprises and was now a strong figure in the area. His letter had stated firmly, "It is about time you did something with the land that Appah left for you. I have taken care of it all these years and it is in good condition. However, it is lying bare next to my house and I have had several offers to buy it. You can build a comfortable house on it and spend your retirement here. I don't suppose your son will be interested in it?"

Retirement, yes, thought Kumaran as the plane shuddered a little and began to lift. And his son, Rudy, for sure would not want his birthright in Jaffna. His son had been given a proper Jaffna name, Rudran, but had come to be known by all as Rudy. Rudy's mother, Manju, was an Indian whom Kumaran had met in graduate school, a Punjabi, strong in mind and body, and a mathematician. She had obtained her doctorate in statistics and gone to work for the Bureau of Labour Statistics. She had now left him and joined an ashram in India, at a place called Cherry. Holy men claimed her totally—her body, mind, and soul. Rudy had married an American girl—indeed, the quintessential American beauty—long-stemmed, blonde, and blue-eyed. *No,* Kumaran said to himself, *Rudy would not be interested in the land that belonged to his ancestors.* Kumaran decided the only course would be to give it to his brother's son. He was the natural heir to the birthright, after Rudy.

The plane circled over the airport and prepared to land. He looked over the coconut palms waving in the breeze and felt a small stirring of nostalgia. It was only when he collected his overnight bag, descended from the plane's ladder, and felt the hot humid air of Colombo embrace him that a sense of loss overcame him. He'd abandoned this sensuous and warm atmosphere that always reached out in this intimate and inviting way. His neighbour on the plane had remarked on the beauty of Lanka. For him and hundreds of other tourists, the beauty was in the cooler reaches of the hill country and the sandy beaches in the western and southern coasts of the island. Kumaran, however, felt at home in the humidity of Colombo in July and looked forward to the heat of the plains in Jaffna.

He walked towards the immigration counter at the newly built airport and stood patiently in line. Ahead of him waited a young man in a white tunic-shirt and slacks. At the desk the young man was asked how much money he had, and he produced a suitcase full of bills.

"Ten thousand dollars," he said. It appeared from the conversation that he was a Lankan who had been working in Dubai for a number of years and was now returning home and who either had no trust in banks or did not want to pay the commission that the banks charged was bringing all of his worldly goods in currency notes.

"Good thing you didn't lose it in transit," the officer remarked dryly as he took him to an adjoining room to have the notes counted.

At last, Kumaran was through customs and immigration. He had finally come home, on an American passport with a Lankan visa, and his brother-in-law, Navam; sisters, Sumi and Devi; and a nephew and a niece were there to meet him. Navam was fatter, balder, and greyer than he had been the last time he had seen him, and was saying something about a station wagon as he hefted the suitcases. Kumaran, however, was studying his nephew and niece. His nephew was now sixteen and growing into a lean and wiry young man. He was dressed in blue jeans and a white shirt. His niece was a year older than his nephew, and she was dressed the same way.

"Blue jeans? How come everyone is dressed in blue jeans?"

"That is the fashion here," his niece said. "So you have come, after all. We thought we were never going to see you."

She was named Revati, but at her insistence, everyone called her Ray. She had become an attractive and bubbly young woman, free and easy in her manner and movements.

"Why did you think that? I had to come sooner or later." Kumaran turned to his nephew, Jana, and asked, "And how old are you? You are growing fast," though he knew how old his nephew was.

"Sixteen," Jana replied, and then remained silent as they made their way through the noisy and cavernous halls of the airport to the parking areas.

His sisters had grown fatter, but they did not look any older, merely a little riper than before. Sumi, the elder of the two, was in her middle forties, and Devi was two years younger. Sumi was a paediatrician at the government hospital and was doing well in her profession. Her husband was also a doctor, and between them, they had built a comfortable life. Ray was their only child. Devi was widowed. She taught in the local school. It was a difficult and demanding job, but it kept her busy. She, too, had only one child—the boy Jana. She had rejected offers to marry again and had chosen to live alone and raise her son.

The station wagon that his brother-in-law drove was roomy enough to carry the large number of welcomers and all the suitcases. The driver manoeuvred it expertly from the airport into the city.

Kumaran looked out of the window and asked, "Why did you all come to the airport?" Though he knew the answer, he also knew that they would give a casual and inaccurate reply.

"Oh, we needed to see you as soon as possible," Devi said, laughing. "We couldn't wait." But Kumaran knew that they had all come to meet him because that was the way to show him their respect and affection. It was the right thing to do.

"I hope you don't mind," said Sumi. "We won't come next time, if you don't want us to."

"No, no. It is quite alright. As long as you don't bring garlands and oil lamps." He had seen such a welcoming ceremony at the Madras airport.

"Why would we do that?" Devi asked.

Kumaran described the ceremony he had seen in Madras. A whole village seemed to have turned out to welcome a young man who was dressed in a well-tailored suit of English cut and style. The young man's relatives and friends were dressed in the Indian fashion. Two females in colourful silk sarees, properly bejewelled and decorated, had held a small tray with a burning wick on it and twirled it around his face, and one of them had collected some red powder from the tray and put a mark on his forehead. This ceremony of welcome and blessing is not performed in Lanka except at weddings. However, Kumaran realized that, oil lamp and tray or not, he was part of a ceremony.

They reached Sumi's house. It was a compact two-story structure with a neat flower garden in front. White jasmine was in full bloom and threw its scent around rather flagrantly, while the few rosebushes seemed to be struggling merely to stay alive.

"You have lost a lot of hair," Devi said as they went into the house. "But you are thinner, I think."

"Perhaps," Kumaran agreed. "Healthy living."

"So how is Manju?" Sumi asked as they walked into the living room. "Tell us about her."

"She is alright," Kumaran said, with what he hoped was nonchalance.

Under her breath, Sumi muttered, "So you did go and see her?"

"I did go to the ashram, and I saw her, for sure. But I am not sure that I understood anything she said."

Sumi and Devi looked at him with knitted brows. They knew, of course, that Manju had left him and become a *sannyasi*, a Hindu nun. He continued, "I saw her and spoke to her. She gave me long philosophical lectures."

Sumi then immediately asked, "Didn't she ask about Rudran?"

"No, she is a complete sannyasi now. She has no interest in her son."

"Well, then," Devi said, "we will have to find you a nice girl here and marry you off." Everyone laughed, somewhat nervously, because they knew about Susan. At first, his family had referred to Susan as his mistress, but he had by now managed to get them to say "friend" or even "Susan, Kumaran's girlfriend."

"Where is Susan now?" Sumi asked.

These questions and the mention of Susan's name suddenly sobered the assembly. Some of the group looked uncomfortable, but his teenage niece giggled.

"Oh, she is in New York," Kumaran said. "She will be joining me in a month." There was a very palpable silence and furtive glances between his sisters at this.

At last, Sumi asked, "Joining you here in Colombo?"

Without expression, Kumaran replied, "Yes. Here. But we will stay in a hotel."

Navam, Sumi's husband, who had been dealing with the driver of the wagon and supervising the unloading of Kumaran's suitcases, entered the room and asked, "Who is going to stay in a hotel?"

Sumi explained the situation to him, and he agreed that it would be better for Susan and Kumaran to move into a hotel after she arrived.

"Why is she coming to Colombo?" Devi asked.

"Just to visit," Kumaran said. "I thought I could bring her here and show her the sights. I thought we might go to Nuwara Eliya and places upcountry."

"Not to Jaffna, then?" Devi asked.

"No, I don't think so. She will join me after I return from Jaffna."

"That's a relief, at least," Sumi said.

The happy warmth of the arrival now seemed to have dissipated a little after the mention of Susan's impending visit.

"Don't worry," Kumaran said. "She may not come at all. When I left, she had not quite made up her mind."

"Let us hope so," Sumi said. She then asked her servant to serve lunch.

After lunch, Kumaran went to his room, unpacked his suitcases, and retrieved the gifts he had purchased for his nephew and niece. As he gave them to the children, he realized that he had made a major error. He had not brought gifts for his sisters. Older as they were, and no doubt wiser, they still expected gifts from him whenever he returned from America. He quickly remarked, "I thought I would buy you some silk sarees in Madras, but after my meeting with Manju, I completely forgot about it. I am sure I can buy some here."

"No, no, you don't have to buy them," Devi responded with a laugh. "Give us the money and we will buy them."

Sumi readily agreed with this suggestion as they watched Ray and Jana unwrap their gifts. The clothes were American and considered fashionable, and the electronic games he'd brought for them were also well received. To his brother-in-law, Navam, he was able to give a shirt that he had bought for himself.

Kumaran decided to go for a walk in the afternoon as his sisters retired for their afternoon nap, a common custom of the leisure classes on weekends. The heat of the afternoon sun was intense as Kumaran trod the pavement, looking into the shops and watching the people amble along. The traffic seemed heavier now, and there seemed to be more vehicles. Strangely enough, the vehicles moved faster and the drivers seemed to be indifferent to most of the rules, while the people moved along on the sidewalk seemingly at peace with themselves.

In spite of all the frustrations caused by the topic of Manju upon his arrival in Colombo, Kumaran felt neither drained nor tired; he did not even feel the jet lag that was supposed to disorient travellers. Perhaps he had returned his body to a time setting of his earlier years. Maybe when he returned to New York, it would hit him.

The next morning, Kumaran decided that this time, he must take possession of the city by himself. He refused Navam's offer to drive him wherever he wanted to go and rejected his nephew's wish to accompany him. Instead he walked to the nearest bus stop.

He arrived at the bank, and it took him more than half an hour to cash his traveller's checks. He finally emerged and walked to the bookstore close by. The bookstore was a good place to begin, a good place to find out what his compatriots were writing, reading, and thinking. He found the section devoted to books on Lanka. There seemed to be a profusion of them—history, anthropology, politics, poetry, and fiction. He bought a dozen or so, and some periodicals, and walked over to the Government Secretariat building.

The Government Secretariat was the hub of the administrative system of the country, and Kumaran was sure that one or more of his friends must be holding powerful positions there. He was looking at the directory in the ground floor of the building when a voice hailed him with his campus nickname. He turned around and saw his old friend, Lalith, advancing towards him with a broad smile on his face. Lalith had been with him at the University in Peradeniya. Later, he'd joined the civil service and had recently become the head of some department or another.

"So, you are back," Lalith said. "Slumming, eh?"

"Yes, I am back. Looking around, touching bases."

"Touching bases, eh? Come on up, let's go to my office." Lalith led the way to the elevator and to his office on the seventh floor.

"Touching bases?" he said again. "Have you also become a baseball fan, then?"

"No, no, it is just an expression."

Lalith sat behind his enormous desk and ordered his office boy to bring tea for the two of them. He picked up the phone and gave some instructions to his secretary in the outer office. Kumaran recognized the morning rituals of the Lankan higher civil servant. Lalith finally turned to Kumaran and asked, "So, how long are you hoping to stay here?"

"For a month or so. I haven't been here for several years. So much seems to have changed."

"Changed? For the better, I hope?"

The higher civil servants in Lanka were a very powerful and privileged group. Though the country was a parliamentary democracy with ministers in charge of running it, they depended on these civil servants to manage the country on a day-to-day basis. Lalith's question, then, was not a mere conversational sally; it was, rather, an invitation to comment on the way he and his colleagues were governing things. Lalith was, in fact, asking for approval of the changes that he and his colleagues had introduced, so Kumaran said guardedly, "There seems to be general liveliness around—at least in the city." This was true. The last time he was in Colombo, there had been a sense of gloom and pessimism.

"A *liveliness*? Come on, fellow, there is a resurgence in the economy! No shortages, no starvation, no queues."

"Yes, that is so," Kumaran conceded, not wanting to get into an argument at that moment. He however added "Except in Jaffna, I suppose." He changed the subject. "How are your children doing? You have two sons, if I remember correctly."

"Yes and no," Lalith said. "I have a daughter as well. They are doing well. The eldest fellow just matriculated. I am sending him to the UK"

"Why the UK?"

"Well, you know, the standards at the university here are terrible. My son wants to study science in the English medium and it is better if he goes abroad." Kumaran wondered how anyone in Lanka could afford to maintain a student overseas on a civil service salary. He also wondered why those who ran the country, like Lalith, were not trying to improve the quality of the education. Lalith was running on about the failures of the educational system, and he attributed it all to the changeover to the national languages as the medium of instruction. A century and half of education in the English medium had been replaced by the national languages. Generally speaking, Lalith was eloquent in his praise of the "changes" in Lanka, but by sending his son to the UK for his collegiate education, he seemed to undermine them as well.

"Come for dinner on Saturday. We will get some old friends together. Whom do you want to meet? Anyone in particular?"

"I don't know. I don't remember who lives in Colombo anymore. Most people I used to know are in Bangkok, Manila, or Geneva or Sydney—not to speak of New York." Kumaran was thinking of the places where the headquarters of the various international organizations were located, in which the senior civil servants, the most efficient or the best connected, had found berths at the peak of their careers.

"Yeah," Lalith said. "Tripping is a way of life here, short trips and long trips. Fly the third world flag, see the world, and give your children a European education. In any case, we will find some old friends. Be there at 7:30."

Kumaran remembered that one of Lalith's close friends, Vim, used to be friendly with him, too. "Whatever happened to Vim?" he asked. "Why don't you get him to come?"

Lalith looked at him, surprised, and said, "Didn't you know? He died a couple of years ago in an accident. He'd been drinking."

So Vim is dead. Kumaran silently recorded this fact, the first death of a friend he had heard of this time, but knowing for certain that there would be more.

"What about Leslie? Do you think he will want to come?" Kumaran asked.

"I don't think so. He and I had a fight."

"Oh, no! What happened? A professional quarrel?" Since the two were both members of the very competitive civil service where overambitious men contended for promotions, this was a plausible surmise.

"Yes, I suppose, you can call it that. It began as one, but it also turned political and ideological later."

"Political? Ideological?"

"I don't want to talk about it. It is too complicated. And, in any case, he is not in Colombo at the moment. He is away in Geneva—some human rights conference or other. He is very busy with that sort of thing. He resigned from the civil service, after the last ethnic riots." Lalith seemed anxious to change the subject, and asked Kumaran about his plans while in Lanka.

Kumaran replied only, "I am going to Peradeniya first and then to Jaffna." Peradeniya was the seat of the country's premier university from which Kumaran and Lalith had graduated.

"To Jaffna?" Lalith said in alarm. "Why to Jaffna? It is not very safe to go there, you know. The troubles are becoming more serious every day."

"The troubles? Is that what they are? Why not call it a civil war?"

"Yes, I suppose that's what we should call it. We do not want to acknowledge it hereabouts. We would rather call it 'terrorism' or 'troubles.' Where do you stand on this?"

"More to the point, where do *you* stand on this?" Kumaran replied. "After all, you live here, help run things, and you are a Sinhalese and a Buddhist."

"I am not sure where I stand on this anymore. Some years ago, I was sure we were doing the right thing, pushing nationalism and cultural revival. Now, I am not so sure."

"One group's nationalism becomes another group's ethnic discrimination," Kumaran noted, somewhat sternly.

"The fact is, I don't know where I stand either," said Lalith. "I have not even been able to digest the concept of a separation of the country into a Sinhalese state and a Tamil state. It feels like an amputation to me. I have grown so used to Lanka as a whole."

"I think this has been coming for a long time. When the British left, we seemed to be a united country, but that was in 1948, and now things seem to have become impossible for the Tamils."

Lalith was not able to accept this. "No, Kum. There is nothing inevitable about it. We will manage; we will change the tide. You will see. The worst is over."

"I hope so, I hope so."

"Are you going home now? I will tell my chauffeur to drive you home."

Kumaran declined the offer and said he had to do some shopping. He left Lalith's office and walked towards the government-run emporium that sold objects made by Lankan craftsmen and craftswomen. It was filled with woodcarvings, brightly coloured batik works, brassware of astonishing variety, and mats with intricate designs made with dried grass. He thought of buying some small objects to take back to America, but changed his mind. Susan was not likely to appreciate them, he felt sure, and they would merely accumulate dust in some closet.

He hailed a taxi and went back to his sister's house, feeling vaguely disturbed.

His sister, Sumi, was a domineering woman who tried to boss everyone around her and manage their lives. She seemed to take after their Aunt Ranie, except that Sumi tended to be more subtle and delicate in her manoeuvres. Sumi was younger than Kumaran, but this did not prevent her from trying to guide his life in ways she deemed appropriate.

"When do you want to go to Jaffna?" she asked that night at dinner. She had invited Devi and her son, Jana, to join them. Kumaran realized that this was not an ordinary evening of a family eating together, and also that the welcoming ceremonies were over.

Devi did not want to waste any time getting to the point. "You had better take possession of the land that Appah left you. You can even get an architect to design a house and ask Shan to start building it." Devi was always a very practical woman, always direct in her declarations.

"Yes," Sumi continued. "You can build a house now and come and live there after your retirement." They all knew that since he was working for the UN, he would have to retire at sixty, in four years' time.

"Yes," Kumaran said, without enthusiasm. "I suppose I can do that. I am glad that Shan has taken the big house."

Shan's possession of the house that his father built on their ancestral property where they had all grown up was only proper, since he was the only one of the four children who was planning to live in Jaffna.

"Yes, yes," Sumi said. "Appah wanted you to have it to begin with, but after you settled down in America, he gave it to Shan."

"You mean after I married Manju," Kumaran said.

"True," Devi said. "After you married Manju, we knew you didn't need a house in Jaffna."

"What about this anniversary rite I have to do?" Kumaran asked.

"Shan performed the funeral rites, even though it was your duty as the firstborn to do it," Sumi said. "But we decided that you must have some part in the final rites to Appah, so we kept some of the ashes for you."

Although Kumaran had a vague idea of such proceedings, he asked, "What do I have to do?"

"You, Shan, and Shan's son will take the urn to the sea at Keerimalai and immerse it in the waters," Sumi said. "I am sure you know that."

They were all silent for a while. Revati, Sumi's daughter, tried to break the silence. "Why do you have to live in America all the time? You can come home now."

"Yes, Maama," added Jana, using the proper kin term. "Come back. We need you here."

"Yes, Revati is right," Devi said. "There is no point in staying in America in your old age."

Sumi joined in. "You must have enough money now."

Navam, Sumi's husband, had remained silent while his wife and sister-in-law tried to convince Kumaran to see things their way. He finally said in rather quiet, measured tones, "You can get married again, you know. You *must* get married. Fifty-five is not too old for a man."

Things were becoming a bit intense for Kumaran. "Leave me alone," he pleaded. "I really don't know what to do. I do not know where I will live after retirement."

"Okay, okay," Sumi said. "Take your time. Anyway, Auntie Ranie will be here tomorrow." Sumi's tone was somewhat ominous, but Kumaran chose not to acknowledge it. Ranie was his mother's sister and her tendency to seek control of the lives of her kin was well known.

"As for the land," Kumaran continued, "I am thinking about giving it to Rajan, Shan's son. He is the one entitled to it, since he is the heir in the male line after Rudy."

"I suppose that is the best thing you can do, since you don't want to live in Jaffna and Rudy does not want it," Sumi said.

"Don't do anything now," Devi insisted. "Wait till you retire. Anything could happen in five years."

"Yes," Navam agreed, "you may change your mind and want to come back and live here."

"You are all forgetting that I have interests and commitments in America, too," Kumaran said, in what he hoped was a calm tone. They all fell silent at that, and it was left to Revati to put into words what they were all thinking.

"You can give her up," she said. Teenager though she was, she was no romantic.

"Yes, why not?" Navam put in. "After all, you are not married to her. Mistresses are not like wives, you know."

"Oh, no," Sumi exclaimed. "How can you say such a thing? Susan is his family. He is no doubt fond of her."

"Thank you, Sumi," Kumaran said. "Lovers are harder to get rid of than wives, because our ties to them are emotional and not legal."

Looking embarrassed, Navam said, "Then you must marry her and bring her with you to Lanka."

"Yes, I suppose I can do that. I will file the necessary papers to divorce Manju when I get back. I am sure she will not raise any objections."

"Yes, Maama," Revati said. "Bring Susan and live here. Life is so pleasant here, in spite of our problems."

That night Kumaran could not fall asleep for a long time. The hot, humid air of Colombo that had seemed to embrace him so warmly when he stepped out of the plane the previous day had now become clammy and stifling, and it kept him turning and tossing. Why had so many decisions been forced on him at this time?

ॐ

Lalith had invited about twenty people to the dinner party, and by the time Kumaran arrived, most of them were already there. He walked onto the front lawn and found many men assembled there with glasses in their hands. It was a pleasantly cool evening, with a breeze blowing from the sea into the house. The women were all congregated on the veranda, earnestly talking to each other. This segregation of the sexes was quite common, even in the sophisticated circles in Colombo, and Kumaran reflected that it was not uncommon in sophisticated campus circles in the States, either.

Lalith took him around and Kumaran tried to remember names and faces. He hadn't seen some of them for over twenty years. There was the short one, who was now also fat and bald. He looked vaguely familiar as he advanced towards Kumaran with a toothy grin, but Kumaran could not quite place him. Kumaran smiled vacantly and was pretending to remember him when Lalith came to his rescue.

"You remember Krishnan, of course," said Lalith.

"Of course," said Kumaran as he shook Krishnan's hand. "So, how are you, Krishnan, old chap? You must be a senior lawyer by now."

"Yes, senior enough," Krishnan said. "I'm managing to survive in the midst of all the chaos."

Then, there was Samaray. He had become a businessman after he left the university, and had prospered. He had, in fact, taken over his father's soap manufacturing business and expanded it into a major house.

"So, Samaray," Kumaran said, laughing, "I have wanted to see you for a long time. Who would have thought that you would become such a successful businessman?"

Samaray was not embarrassed in the least by this veiled allusion to his youth. It had been a youth full of promise, but of literature and writing, not of money and commerce. He had been reading English at the campus and was already publishing poetry. An excellent student, he seemed destined to obtain a good degree and move effortlessly into a distinguished academic career. He had also been an excellent actor and had graced many of the university dramatic society's plays with his commanding presence. Samaray had also been passionately in love with a fellow student named

Rex, a delicate and soft-spoken Eurasian boy from Galle. In his final year, Samaray's father died of a heart attack, and Samaray seemed to undergo a radical transformation. He abandoned his studies, his poetry, drama, and even Rex, and he became serious and thoughtful, in his way. After the end of the first term of his final year, he never came back to finish his degree. He took over his father's business and managed it on his own. Then he married and eventually became a successful tycoon.

Now, here he was, in Lalith's house, still recognizably himself—slim, tall, and graceful, full of courtesy and manners. "So, Kumaran," Samaray began. "Here you are, after all these years. I hear you have come back to settle down."

"I don't know, Samaray. I don't know what I want to do yet." Having said that, Kumaran wondered how Samaray knew that he had returned to settle in Lanka. It was a strange thing for anyone to know, since he had not told anyone nor given it much thought.

Param, who had joined the national police force as soon as he had graduated and risen to be head of intelligence, was getting drunk. He asked Kumaran a question that many in the group wanted to ask but were too tactful to raise.

"How about your old flame, Sujata? Are you going to see her?" Param asked mockingly.

"No," said Kumaran. "I haven't seen her in inh several years."

"You know, her husband left her—or she left her husband," Param continued. "Terrible drunk he turned out to be."

Kumaran had indeed heard this story about his old sweetheart. He had often thought about her, but had avoided making any contact with her after he left the campus so many years earlier. Now that Param had opened the subject, others were ready to make their own contributions. Param gave a vivid portrait of Sujata's present circumstances. She had become the director of cultural programs for the government radio system and was apparently responsible for many innovations. Her public life was very successful, but her private life was a total disaster. She had married an officer in the army soon after she left the campus, they had two children in rapid succession, and then the marriage began to flounder.

"Are you going to see her?" Now it was Samaray's turn to ask this question.

"Perhaps I will. Who knows?" Kumaran said with a laugh, and tried to change the subject. But Param was not easily diverted.

"She knows you are here. My wife is a friend of hers." Kumaran was wondering how to respond to this when Lalith, thankfully, began to talk about cricket.

"You never played cricket in England, did you?" he asked. Kumaran had been an outstanding cricketer in his school days.

"No, I gave up cricket after Peradeniya. My purpose in London was exclusively academic."

The next thing Kumaran said was the right question: "Who will win the match this year?" He knew that to some in the crowd assembled there, this question would not make any sense. To many others, however, it could refer only to the contest for cricket supremacy between their old school and its rival. This old school, a high school at that, had a special place in their lives and in the life of the country. The children of the elite went there in addition to others who were admitted based on talent. Eventually, the students became the elite and, in turn, ran the country. Nevertheless, the topic did not move a few. Vivek was there and could abide neither cricket nor the old school ties.

"Ah, come on, Kumaran," he said. "I thought after all these years abroad, you would have grown out of these things."

"Oh, I have," Kumaran assured him readily. "I was merely making conversation."

Param looked hard at Vivek and interjected, "You were always a spoilsport. If I remember right, you were the only one from our class who never went to a single cricket match."

"Yes, I claim that distinction," Vivek said, beaming. He had been a radical then, reading advanced socialist literature and making speeches at the slightest provocation. He had organized a small political cell in the school too and tried to publish a weekly newspaper with red letters in the title. It did not last more than a term. He was still a radical, but was not active politically. He had become an accountant for a firm. He kept his radical credentials by making financial contributions to the leftist political parties.

Everyone had a tale to tell and an anecdote to recount. It was the financially and professionally successful lot out of their crowd who were at the party, Kumaran concluded, and he wondered about the others. There was, he remembered, Nathan. He too had gone abroad, to Nigeria or Zambia, to teach. After a couple of years, he had come back, married his cousin, and taken her abroad with him. He'd eventually taken his own life, and his wife and son had come back to Lanka destitute and impoverished.

Samaray interrupted this reverie. "What are you going to do while in Lanka?"

Kumaran had planned the days he'd spend on the island in great detail. He was going to reach as many of the places as he could manage, stay there for a few days, and move on to others. He would go to those places that had a niche in his memory so as to reappropriate them, as well as to places he had never visited but wanted to appropriate now. This land he had abandoned, or that had abandoned him, carelessly and thoughtlessly, he wanted to acquire now, at least for his memory, and take it with him to his new home. He did not tell all this to Samaray, but said instead, "I want to visit some places, you know. I am going to Peradeniya to visit the campus. Spend a couple of days there. You remember Wijay. He asked me to give a talk there."

"Yes, I know Wijay," Samaray replied. "He is head of the economics department now, isn't he?"

"Yes, I will spend a few days there and then go to some places upcountry," said Kumaran. Upcountry was the term the British used in Lanka to describe the hilly middle section of the island where the climate was cool and wet and the tea grew in luxuriant abundance. "You know, I have never been upcountry, all these years."

"No?" Param interposed. "That's very strange. I know a tea plantation there where you can stay."

Kumaran declined the offer, but wrote down the name of the owner anyway, in case he became stranded. He did not want to stay in those estate bungalows. He'd heard that they were damp and dingy, and he preferred to stay in the local guesthouses. These guesthouses and small hotels had become quite commonplace since European and American tourists started coming to the island.

"After the upcountry?" Samaray asked.

"I am going to the wildlife sanctuary at Wilpatu and then home to Jaffna."

It was only after the last phrase left his mouth that Kumaran realized how strange it must have sounded. He had no home in Jaffna. He was only going to stay with his brother for a few weeks. But Samaray and Param did not see anything strange in his remark and continued asking their questions.

"You will come back to Colombo and then leave from here?" Param asked. "There are some other buggers you must see before you go. I will get them together when you come back to my place. My wife may get Sujata to come too."

There'd always been a gathering of friends when Kumaran returned to the island in the past. One of his friends would organize a party, invite people he knew in his youth, and others as well, and they would drink and talk well into the night. Perhaps the fact that Kumaran had become an eminent international civil servant brought all these people together. Kumaran also knew, though, that Lankans had a gift for friendship. Living amidst all manner of people in the UN community, he had not come across such a capacity to remember and cherish old friends as among the Lankans.

∾

Sumi woke Kumaran the next morning with the news that Auntie Ranie was on her way. She was his mother's younger sister and lived in Badulla, a city in the central highlands located one hundred and fifty miles from Colombo. She was coming to see Kumaran, and this did not make him particularly happy. He did not like his Auntie Ranie, but the auntie did not seem to realize this. She had always blundered on, as was her way, and sought to envelop him in her plans and projects, which usually involved marriage for someone, and although Kumaran was now past his prime, he felt sure that Auntie Ranie had heard about Manju's departure and was ready with new proposals. Nothing daunted Auntie Ranie. She was always trying to marry him off. Even while he was preparing to leave for the USA, she had come forth with marriage propositions for him. He had somehow negotiated himself out of them, with the help of his father. Nevertheless, she continued to plague him. He could not remember whether any of the women were suitable, even in the loose sense in which the word was used in Lanka. More often than not, people arranging marriages sought to enforce their own view of the fitness of things or perhaps even maliciously sought to create sorrow for the candidates by bringing incompatible people together. Auntie Ranie was not malicious, only rather silly, and not given to deep reflection or thought.

She arrived a little later in the morning, bustling and noisy as ever, in a rickety taxi from the railway station. Since she hadn't told anyone exactly when she was coming, no one had met her.

Sumi was fond of Ranie in her way, and made up for the absence of honours at the station by fussing over her now. She showed her to her room, gave her breakfast, and made all the polite inquiries about her children. Ranie had an unmarried daughter living with her at home and a son who was working as a teacher in Jaffna. Aunt Ranie's major worry in life was the daughter. She lost no time in coming to the point, even as she devoured the steaming hoppers that Sumi placed in front of her.

"Thambi," she said, addressing Kumaran by the familiar kinship term, "you must know some good men for my Santi. Someone in America. Why don't you arrange something for her?" Kumaran was relieved that she had not come with some widow or divorcée for him this time.

"Yes, Auntie," Kumaran said, but without much enthusiasm. "I will look around."

"Don't just say it like that," Auntie Ranie retorted, sensitive to every nuance and colour in conversations and recognizing Kumaran's indifference. "You must try hard. There are no suitable young men here now. They have all gone to America, the UK, Australia, or the Middle East, and when they come back, they ask for huge dowries."

"Yes, Auntie! I will keep it in mind. I can't think of anyone now. My friends—the Lankan ones—don't have any sons, but I will look around."

"If only your mother were alive, I am sure she would force you to help your cousin. My Santi is a pretty girl, as you know, and she is already twenty-five, but I can't settle her. She has a B.A., too."

"I told you, Auntie. I will try. I will do my best, I promise."

"She is a very modern girl. She will make a good wife, even in America."

"Yes, Auntie."

"Now," Auntie Ranie said with a softer tone, "I have not forgotten my responsibility to you. You married that Indian woman and got into all this trouble. If you had only listened to me . . . So what are you going to do now?"

Auntie Ranie had never found it possible to call Manju by name. Whenever Kumaran brought her to Colombo, Auntie Ranie avoided meeting her and always referred to her as "that Indian woman." The fact that he had married an Indian, even an impeccable Hindu of high caste, had not appeased many of his relatives. For them, anyone who was not from their own community and caste was a foreigner and an outsider. When he had left for the US for the first time, their worry was that he would marry an American and bring disgrace to the clan. Kumaran had expected them to be relieved that he had married an Indian. Everyone except his father, mother, and brother and sisters had been disturbed by the marriage. Auntie Ranie had gone further—she had predicted disaster. She now felt triumphant and was prepared to overlook the fact that he and Manju had remained more or less happily married for over twenty years. Auntie Ranie did not know of his arrangements with Susan. She kept talking.

"The Judge sent a message to me last week," she said. "His daughter is a widow. Her husband died two years ago—they had no children. She must be about thirty-five years old or so."

Sumi could not contain herself at this point. "Oh, no, Auntie," she said. "She was my classmate. She must be at least forty-two years old."

"Okay, okay," Auntie conceded. "What is a few years at this stage?" She looked meaningfully at Kumaran. "What you need now is a companion. I think you should see her."

Kumaran smiled at this familiar marriage broker pitch and waited for the rest.

"She comes from a respectable family. They have land, money, and position."

She rambled on, and Kumaran wondered whether he should tell her about Susan. How would he put it to her? What was the correct description of Susan? Companion, friend, lover? Whatever he called her, he was sure Auntie Ranie would call her his mistress or concubine. Yet he was sure that she had heard about the relationship and was studiously ignoring it. After all, she knew that most men have affairs and mistresses at one time in their lives, and this had nothing to do with a marriage at all. Her husband, a teacher in Kandy, was a meek and gentle person, completely under Aunt Ranie's control, and Kumaran felt sure he had never had an affair or a mistress.

"Okay," said Kumaran. "I will think about it. How can I avoid it? A girl from a respectable, wealthy family with position in society? A judge's daughter?"

Auntie Ranie looked at him suspiciously. "I suppose that will do for now. What are you doing now—I mean, when are you going to Jaffna? You can see the girl then."

"Okay, okay," Kumaran replied. "I am going to the university in Peradeniya in a day or two. I have to give a talk there. I will probably go to Jaffna after that."

"And when are you going back to America?" Auntie Ranie was ever mindful of the days, weeks, and months that were necessary to arrange a marriage and a wedding. "If you like the judge's daughter, we can have the wedding here before you leave."

"Oh, no, it can't work like that. I only said that I will think about it."

"You are not going back to India, again? There is no point, Thambi. That is over, and thank your stars. It is best to stick to our people."

"Yes, Auntie, that's true. I am not going back to India again, no."

"Now, I must do some shopping," Auntie Ranie said with the air of a woman who had accomplished a mission of some importance. "I will take Revati and go to Kundanmall's. I want to buy some sarees for Santi."

"I will come too," Sumi said.

"Me too," Devi said.

As they were getting ready to leave, Kumaran drew Sumi aside and gave her some money, saying, "Buy a saree for Shanti too, and give it to Auntie."

II

NEW YORK

KUMARAN'S RECOLLECTIONS OF HIS trip to India and Cherry were not too pleasant. His wife, Manju, had moved into an ashram in Cherry. She had severed all connections with him and their son Rudy except for a couple of letters.

Kumaran had met Manju during his first semester at the University of Wisconsin in Madison, at the Thanksgiving family dinner to which the dean of foreign students had arranged to have them both invited. In the first year of a foreign student's term in America, the authorities in the universities take some interest in the student's social life. During the anxious early months, some foreign students would not know enough people with whom they could celebrate holidays, so the dean's office would step in. Mrs. Hudson, Kumaran's appointed hostess, had telephoned him at his dormitory, and after the usual preliminaries, asked, "Will you be picking up Manju, or do you need a ride?"

"Manju?"

"Manju," Mrs. Hudson replied, forming the word with some difficulty. "She is coming to Thanksgiving dinner with you. Didn't the dean's office call you?"

"They did, but they didn't say anything about Manju."

"That's alright, then. Do you have a car, or shall we pick you up?"

Kumaran did not have a car. It was already cold in Madison, and as he sat in Mr. Hudson's car, he could see snow piled up high on the sidewalks. They picked up Manju on the way. She was wrapped in a fake fur coat and wearing a woollen hat. Mr. and Mrs. Hudson and their son, Jerry, greeted the two newcomers at their front door.

"My daughter, Debra, couldn't make it this year," Mrs. Hudson said. "She has a serious case of the flu."

"That's too bad," Manju said. "I was looking forward to meeting her."

"I am sure she will be here for Christmas, and you can meet her then."

The mulled wine, warm and smelling of cinnamon and cloves, was exactly what Kumaran needed. Despite the tweed jacket and lamb's wool pullover he was wearing, he was shivering.

"I still haven't gotten used to the cold," he told Mrs. Hudson. "I don't know when I will."

Mrs. Hudson looked at him kindly, led him to the picture window in the living room, and asked him to look out.

"You must go with the cold," she said. "You must not fight it. I think you and Jerry should put on some skis and do some cross-country skiing."

"Perhaps now?" said Jerry, coming over to join them at the window. "We can suit up and do a little run before dinner."

"No, no," Kumaran said in alarm. "Some other time."

Still, he could not help noticing the shimmering beauty of the snow on the lawn and beyond as it lay undisturbed in all its whiteness. It snows like this every year, it gets cold like this every year, and the people who live here manage to stay warm every year too. What a wonderful thing!

"Yes," Kumaran said to Mrs. Hudson, "one must go with the winter, understand it, live with it. I am sure I will, sooner or later."

He returned to his chair and sipped his wine. He looked at Manju closely now as she sat there talking to Mr. Hudson. She was slim as a reed and had a sinuous grace. She was dressed in a light blue *salwar kameez* that set off her golden brown complexion nicely. He felt something stir inside him. As the afternoon progressed, he began to realize that he was being captivated. He noticed the fine symmetry of her face, the dark arched eyebrows, and above all, her easy and fluent laughter. In retrospect, he realized that it was this laughter that had first drawn him in. This discovery only made him very self-conscious. He could not look at Manju anymore, and did not feel he could talk to her without betraying his nervousness. He turned his entire attention to Mrs. Hudson and started flirting and joking with her.

He returned to his dormitory overfed, slightly tipsy, and with a mind full of conflict. He had not felt these romantic stirrings for a long time, not since the fiasco of his relationship with Sujata. Now here was another Sujata! Was it the blue dress, the eyebrows, the slight, diminutive form? What is it about a particular woman that holds a special meaning for a man, whispers the witch's message and draws him into the maze? He fell into a troubled slumber and dreamt of Peradeniya and colourful grass mats and being bowled out in a cricket match in the first ball.

He woke up the next morning considerably calmer and more relaxed and concluded that the wine, the fireplace, and the warmth of the Hudson home had confused him and that he should stop being silly. Falling in love in one's first semester and at first sight? Not to be taken seriously, so he let the matter of Manju drop. He focused on his studies and tried to adjust to a new culture. The best way to do this, he discovered, was to watch the romantic dramas that were broadcast on the television in the afternoon. The subtleties of interpersonal transactions, the rites and customs of American domestic life, were on naked display here, and Kumaran spent his afternoons in the television room of the dormitory absorbing them.

One day late in December, he decided to go to the Christmas concert at the school auditorium. It was organized by the university music department and consisted of both professional and semiprofessional performers. He went to the box office to buy a ticket and felt an acute embarrassment when the clerk raised an eyebrow and asked, "*One* ticket?" He had no date, no friend who could accompany him. He had met many young women, some of them quite likable, but had not cultivated friendships.

He had barely seated himself when he looked around and saw Manju headed towards the seat next to him. After the holiday dinner at the Hudson's, he had seen her off and on the campus at various times and they had chatted. That day, however, Kumaran saw some kind of special providence, before he caught himself and concluded that he and Manju must have bought the only two remaining single tickets, and naturally, they were sold as two adjacent seats. Nevertheless, he decided to make the most of it.

"I had no idea that you were interested in classical music," Manju said as she sat down.

"I do like the vocals," Kumaran replied. "I don't much like the symphonies."

"Then you are in for a treat. Anna Moffo is going to sing some arias, and she is very good. You must learn to like symphonies too. They have an excellent orchestra here. The season will begin next week."

"I may learn to like it if I listen to it, I am sure. How did you get interested in it?"

"I liked the mathematical precision of it, the calculated ratios between the notes."

"Just the technical aspects, then?"

"No, not just those. That was at the beginning. My math professor mentioned it in passing, and I followed it up. And then I got interested in the music as a whole." Her words seemed rushed.

"Well, you must explain it all to me sometime. Since the season is opening next week, we can go to the concert and you can tell me all about it." He had jumped to take the opening that had been offered to him.

Manju laughed at this and said that there was nothing to explain, and that he should just listen and let the music flow into him and over him. "Understanding will come in time," she said. She did agree, however, to go to the concert with him.

It was an easy friendship that developed between them, but Kumaran was reluctant to take it any further. Once again he felt the same diffidence about making the bold move that had afflicted him those long years ago at the university in Peradeniya. Doubts about being able to pull off an intercultural marriage plagued him, and he let matters drift along between him and Manju. And yet they met frequently and went to movies and concerts and worked together on common academic problems. It turned out, however, that Manju was not one to leave matters alone and unresolved.

One day Kumaran was having lunch at the student cafeteria when Professor Rohit Sharma, whom he knew slightly, and was in fact one of Manju's teachers, came and sat down at his table. Sharma was a professor of mathematics, one of the few Indians on the academic staff, and he took a particular interest in the Indians who came under his purview. After a few pleasantries, he began to talk about Manju. He mentioned her family in India and what a good respectable family it was. Since Kumaran already had some inkling of this, he was mystified why the professor was bringing it up. "I understand you have been seeing a lot of her," said the professor.

"Yes, indeed. She is a good friend of mine."

"Yes, I know," said the professor. He then changed the subject. "You will be finishing your PhD soon, won't you?"

"Yes, indeed. I will be defending my dissertation next month."

"And what will you be doing after that?"

"I I have been offered a job in the UN. I'll be doing economic analysis."

"Not going back to Lanka? Perhaps you will be wanting to get married before you get settled in your new job?"

"No, no! I have no such plans. I'm going to New York soon after my defence and taking up the position."

"Perhaps you should get married."

Kumaran was beginning to get both annoyed and a little intrigued by this intrusion into his personal life. Such inquiries were not unusual in Asian society, but here in Wisconsin, to be interrogated by Professor Sharma, who had lived in the United States for several years, was quite unexpected.

The professor, however, continued. "I think you should indeed get married. And I'm here to propose Manju as a good match for you. You know her quite well, and I'm sure she likes you and will be a perfect match."

Kumaran was too astonished to say anything for a while. He stared at Professor Sharma for quite some time and finally said, "My God, you are a marriage broker just like at home and arranging a marriage for me."

"Well, not exactly like at home. I'm more of a messenger than a marriage broker. It was Manju who sent me. She thinks that you like her but are too shy or too frightened about approaching her."

Kumaran's astonishment subsided somewhat, and he replied, "Oh, come on, Professor Sharma. She is a Punjabi Brahmin, and I'm a commoner from Lanka, and surely there is little chance of a marriage working out between us."

Professor Sharma frowned a little. "You're being stupid. This is the twentieth century, and those customs don't operate anymore. And besides, you are in America."

Kumaran went silent, and after a minute or two, told the professor that he would think about it and speak to Manju directly.

He went back to his apartment and waited impatiently for the evening to arrive so that he could call Manju at her dormitory. Kumaran had indeed turned diffident when he thought about approaching her and telling her about his feelings, because he believed that, though they were both from the subcontinent, there certainly were important cultural differences between the beautiful and talented young woman, and a Lankan. He had thought that the marriage between the two would not be feasible. But now that she had expressed interest, he wanted to tell her that he too was interested in marrying her and seeking to bridge the cultural divide between India and Sri Lanka.

When he saw her the next evening he wasted no time in telling her that he was indeed very fond of her but was nevertheless quite surprised at the news that Professor Sharma had given him the previous evening.

He wrote to his mother and father, and to his additional surprise, they did not make any strong objections. After the fiasco of their trying to arrange a marriage for him when he had stopped over in Lanka on his way to Madison from London, they had finally come to accept that it was not possible to arrange a conventional Lankan marriage for Kumaran. They were no doubt relieved that he was, after all, marrying a Hindu.

❦

Kumaran and Manju finished their graduate studies in Wisconsin, he in economics and she in mathematics, and he began working at the United Nations in Manhattan. After a while, Manju joined the Bureau of Labour Statistics, and they found themselves living the lives of affluent expatriates in Westchester, a fashionable suburb of New York City. A whole culture of new Indian, Pakistani, and Lankan immigrants had emerged in New York City and its environs, and Manju and Kumaran fit into this little world without difficulty, in which the regional and religious differences between the various peoples of India were muted, in a search to create a common theme. It was an island in which a certain cultural loneliness that the immigrants experienced was overcome, at least to some degree.

Yet it was not easy living in this artificial community. Kumaran would go to parties with Manju and find himself the only Lankan there. Manju and her friends would jabber away in Panjabi, so Kumaran felt left out.

"A common surface culture," Kumaran remarked to Manju after returning from one such party, "but with internal contradictions."

"What contradictions?"

"Your Panjabi food is different, your religion is different, and we even look different."

"So what do you care? You like the food anyway, and we are not religious at all. You are an atheist, and I think I am too."

"And I don't understand you when you talk in Panjabi," Kumaran continued.

"The same is true when I go to your Lankan parties. You should not mind these differences, Kum; you should learn to enjoy them."

"I do enjoy them, but sometimes, I resent being excluded from the talk."

Manju refused to debate the issue further and walked away. She had a parting shot, however. "Get modern, Kum! We must get modern and ignore our traditional differences."

Rudran was born a couple of years after they moved to New York. He eventually went to a school where he met children of other UN officials from all over the world. There was a mix of cultures, but they all learned in the English medium. Rudy, as he soon came to be called, became a creature of this universal culture and developed a certain indifference to the styles and attitudes of his father and mother. The fact that their common culture was rather tenuous did not help much.

Rudy elected to go to California for his college education. He had obtained admission to Columbia and Princeton as well, but had accepted the offer from Berkeley. Kumaran suspected that he had decided on California because it was far away from New York, but he never mentioned this to Manju.

After Rudy left, Manju and Kumaran settled into what he thought was a comfortable domesticity. It had been twenty years since they married, and now, they were alone together again.

This soon changed. One day, Manju came home with Susan and cooked dinner for the three of them. Susan had been working with Manju for about a year, and they had quickly become friends. She too, it appeared, was a lost woman, feeling out of place in the city. Slim and tall, with bright blue eyes and long flowing hair, Susan was nevertheless not what would be considered pretty by American standards. She was too thin and flat. But she did have a warmth and a concreteness about her, a presence, an immediacy. She tried hard to create an impression of a certain innocence, but underneath, she was a very determined young woman. She had moved to New York from Springfield, Massachusetts, and joined Manju's office as a junior statistician. She was running away from her family, particularly her father, who, she reported, was a domineering autocrat who bullied her mother and her with a religious zeal. He was quite opposed to Susan obtaining a master's degree in mathematics and kept nagging her to follow a more "suitable" career. The moment she was able to leave home, she did, and she rarely contacted her parents.

Manju brought Susan home to dinner frequently after the first visit, and the three of them became almost inseparable.

Manju would often go on official business to Washington D.C. and ask Susan to come over to cook dinner and keep Kumaran company. Soon, Kumaran found himself slipping, almost without effort, into an affair with Susan. She was at home so often and had become so much a part of the household that it did not even seem illicit to him.

One day, while Manju, Susan, and Kumaran were watching television after dinner, Manju said, almost casually, "Why don't we ask Susan to move in here, permanently? She can have the spare bedroom. It will be good company for you and me."

Kumaran did not react to this in any way except to present a blank stare. In fact, he did not know how to react. That Susan and he were lovers and that Manju was participating in a game of consensual adultery was no longer an issue. But to have Susan move in and create a threesome was something that Kumaran had not thought possible.

Susan was ready with an answer. "Why not?" she said. "It will make everything so simple." Kumaran was not sure whether Susan was being sarcastic. He looked at her closely and could not find any clue. He remained silent.

Manju chimed in. "There is no reason to carry on this game, Kum. I do like having Susan around, and so do you. Susan likes us too, so why not live together?"

Kumaran finally found his voice. "How will we manage? What will we tell people?"

"Don't worry, Kum," Manju said with a twinkle in her eyes. "It will be easy to make the domestic arrangements. It has been done before, you know."

"Yes, yes. I know that it has been done before," Kumaran said. He turned to Susan and asked, "What do you think, Susan? Do you think it will work?"

"It's worth a try. When Manju asked me about it this morning at lunch, I was readily agreeable."

"Oh," Kumaran said, surprised. "You two have already talked about it."

"Of course we have. I love you both, though each in a different way, and can't bear to hurt either of you."

"And we love you too, Susan," Manju interposed. Kumaran could not help noticing the smug expression on Manju's face. It seemed as though she had successfully implemented a coup de grace. Susan looked solemn and continued without acknowledging Manju's interruption.

"It was my affection for Manju that brought me here in the first place. From the time I was in graduate school when Manju came to teach that one course, I began to admire her, and it grew when I began to work for her." She stopped abruptly, realizing that she had perhaps said enough. After a moment of silence, she said, "We can give it a try, anyway, and see where it leads us—the three of us."

"The three of us," Kumaran repeated, who had quickly reconciled to the idea. "Too bad we couldn't have 'the four of us'; then we could play bridge instead of watching TV all the time."

"Well," Manju said, "I will look out for another companion, and if she can play bridge, I will ask her to move in too."

Kumaran laughed, and the remaining tension created by the abrupt transformation of the covert arrangement to an overt one subsided.

They made the necessary arrangements for this new unit of man-with-two-mates living under the same roof, and they became, in time, an interesting, if rather bizarre, threesome. Kumaran lost all embarrassment and shame over it, and in all social occasions, they were recognized as a unit. He would go to concerts, plays, and other performances with Manju and Susan sitting on either side of him. If it raised some eyebrows in the beginning and elicited a few snide remarks about harems, reactions soon subsided, and everyone he knew seemed to accept the situation. Invitations to parties and dinners began to routinely include both Manju and Susan, except for the formal ones. They included only his legal companion's name, and this often meant that, but for the important professional ones, Kumaran declined them.

Kumaran could not remember exactly when the situation began to change again. He realized after a while that Manju was finding one reason or another not to sleep with him. Two years of happy hareming were slowly coming to an end, and about the same time, he began to notice other, minor, signs of her emotional and social withdrawal. She had begun reading philosophy and religion books on Hinduism and Buddhism and returned to her earlier interest in physics and astronomy. It was all very puzzling. She would talk animatedly about the theory of karma, move without a break into quantum physics, and end with statements like, "It depends on us—everything depends on us—on our perceptions—on what we see."

On other occasions, she would say, without any provocation, things like "The end is all . . . it is the finale that matters, how one is to end. The beginning and the middle are merely overtures and can take any form."

Kumaran and Susan would exchange glances whenever Manju delivered these statements, sometimes at appropriate moments in the conversation, and others not. They were once talking about a brutal murder in the city, a murder-suicide, in fact. A middle-aged mother, an immigrant from Manila, had killed her three children and then herself in the east side of New York City. It was an affluent section, and the husband had left them in the morning in apparent normalcy and returned home to find their bodies. It was in the course of this story that Manju had delivered the homily, "The end is all. It is the ending that matters."

"How do you mean? End?" Susan had responded. "Whose end? Matters to whom?"

Manju was unwilling to expand on her remarks, but instead, went into an exposition of the cycle of births and deaths that Hinduism claims is the lot man has in store till total oblivion is reached.

"Death is not the end, unfortunately, as far as one knows. It may only be another beginning," she had said. "Nirvana is the end."

These pronouncements began to take a more coherent form after Manju started going to yoga classes at some centre in the city. She tried to get Susan to go with her, but after one session, she wouldn't go anymore. It soon became apparent that the yoga centre was having some impact on Manju's thinking. One day, the three of them were sitting in the living room, trying to decide where they should go for dinner, when Susan asked, "How are your exercise classes coming along, Manju?"

"They are not exercises," Manju said. "Not *just* exercises."

"No?"

"All life is yoga. Yoga is to be one in body and spirit and understanding."

"How can one become one in body, spirit, and understanding by standing on one's head?" Susan asked.

Manju looked at Susan with what almost seemed to be contempt. "There are many ways. But first, one must abdicate desire. In place of desire, there must be a single-minded aspiration towards the divine."

"How can one do that? Abdicate desire, I mean?" She turned to Kumaran and asked, "Do you understand any of this?"

Kumaran said, "I am beginning to. What Manju means is that we must renounce life and its pleasures."

"Yes, that's part of it," Manju said. "But the renunciation must be done for the right motive."

"And what is the right motive?" Kumaran asked.

"It is too easy to give up things or people and go away. This can come from fear and weakness and can be a mere escape from responsibility. Renunciation must not be for leaving the world, but for joining with God."

"I don't understand any of this," Susan said. "Let us go to dinner. Some place cheery and noisy and full of lights."

"No, no," Kumaran said. "I want to know more about this. This doesn't sound like the usual stuff, this yoga of yours."

"Yes, it is not the exercise business," Manju replied. "This is integral yoga—a synthesis of the physical, mental, devotional."

"Whatever has happened to you, Manju?" Susan said. "I always thought you were a scientist. I can still remember your lectures to us on the logical beauty of mathematics."

"There is beauty everywhere," Manju replied.

"Okay, Manju, I'm hungry. Let's go." Susan left the room and came back with her hat and coat. "No more talk of yoga and renunciation, and karma."

"Yes, let us do that," Manju said, smiling. "No more religious mumbo-jumbo." Yet Kumaran could not help but feel that this cheerfulness was somehow forced.

These changes were gradual and seemed to have been judiciously punctuated. Yet, Kumaran recalled, they had taken on a certain intensity after Rudy's last visit. He had called and said he was coming during the long Thanksgiving holiday weekend, and so Manju had to make some quick arrangements—Susan never went to visit her folks during Thanksgiving, and so she had to be sent to stay with some friends in Long Island. Rudy no doubt knew about Kumaran's unusual domestic situation, but there was no mutual acknowledgement between the two of them.

Rudy had become a very handsome young man—light brown skin with masses of black hair falling down to his shoulders. No doubt it was his awareness of his good looks and a keen intelligence that had given him an overbearing and overconfident personality. He was always blustering about, too sure of himself, too thoroughly insensitive to others.

Manju had prepared chapattis and mutton korma for Rudy. Rudy looked at the food, not too fondly, and remarked, "I haven't eaten this kind of food for a long time."

"Don't you cook Indian food?" Manju asked.

"No," Rudy said curtly. He took a piece of a chapatti, tentatively dipped it in the curry, and put it into his mouth.

"This is too spicy for me," he said, but continued to eat.

"Korma is too spicy for you?" Kumaran said. "It is the mildest curry you can imagine."

"He has become too American," Manju said, a trifle sadly. "He doesn't like anything Indian anymore. I should have made hamburgers."

"Perhaps he doesn't like us either. We are not American enough."

"Don't be silly, Dad," Rudy said.

"Don't call me Dad," Kumaran snapped. "I am *Appa* to you."

They ate silently after that. After a while, Manju began telling Rudy about her jewels. She told him about their history, how her mother and her mother's mother had acquired them and protected and preserved them over the generations and how she was having some difficulty in disposing of them now.

"I am thinking of taking them back to Jalandhar, to India," she concluded, and looked expectantly at Rudy.

Rudy ate silently for awhile and then said, almost casually, "Yes, that's the right thing to do. No one here will want them."

Kumaran did not interfere in this conversation. He ate in silence as mother and son engaged in making various decisions about property, descent, and generations.

"So you don't mind my giving these jewels to your cousin?" Manju said, coming back to the topic after discussing other matters.

"No, not really," Rudy said. "I am sure Carol would have no use for them," nonchalantly introducing the subject of his visit.

Manju flinched a little. "Carol?"

Rudy extracted a picture from his wallet and showed it to Manju. Kumaran walked over and looked at it too. It was a tall, blond woman in jeans and a shirt, smiling happily at the camera.

"Your girlfriend?" Kumaran asked. "She is very pretty."

"My wife, actually. We got married last week."

"Married? Last week?"

"Married?" Manju stared blankly at Rudy and then asked, "And you didn't tell us?"

"It is no big deal, Ma. We just got married at the county clerk's office. We had to do it."

Manju and Kumaran looked at each other, unable to speak. Finally, Manju got up and walked towards her room. As Kumaran stared in disbelief at Rudran, they heard her close the door behind her.

"How could you do such a thing? You could marry anyone you wanted, but not to tell us and make us part of the process is unforgivable."

"I know, Dad, I know. That's why I came this time, to bring you the news personally. We didn't want to wait too long. Carol is pregnant, and she insisted on getting married as soon as possible."

"Yes, yes. Still, there was no need to keep us out of it. Your mother believes in an orderly world, you know."

"Yes," Rudy said.

"Dammit, so do I, come to think of it. I don't want my only son getting married at the courthouse."

"What has happened, has happened. You can come and visit us in Berkeley next summer—Carol and me and, perhaps, your grandson."

Kumaran got up, walked towards Manju's room, and found it locked from the inside.

After Rudy's visit, Manju became more withdrawn and contemplative. It was easy to see that she was undergoing a crisis of some kind. Her passing comments on the nature of human life and experience became more cryptic and aphoristic. One day at dinner, apropos of nothing, or something invisible to Kumaran and Susan, she said, "The universe cannot exist without an observer. Did you know that, Susan? It follows that the objects in the universe cannot exist without an observer. You and Kumaran cannot exist without someone noticing you—in this instance, you cannot exist without me," she concluded with a triumphant air. Then she said, almost to herself, "Conversely, if no one observes me, I don't exist."

Susan had replied immediately, "Oh, come on, Manju, don't lay this stuff on us all the time. I am sick of it. Of course we exist! What are you talking about? This is madness!"

"You have been reading the wrong books," Kumaran said. "Tell us then, what are they?"

"Books? Well, no simple book will answer all questions, Kum. Actors and spectators are not separate in quantum theory. They are part of the same order."

"You mean I cannot see and define an objective world?"

"No, there is no objective world. Everything is made real by our perceptions."

"Says who?" Susan said.

"Come on, Susan," Manju replied. "Don't play dumb. You have studied physics. It was Heisenberg. He said that physics must be confined to a formal description of the relation between perceptions."

"Well, if you want to refer to quantum theory, I can retort that once something is perceived or measured, it becomes stable and objective," Susan observed, deciding not to play dumb anymore.

"True enough. One can nevertheless continue to introduce new perceptions and dissolve the objective world. I want to become the unobserved one, the nonexistent thing."

"You mean, you want to dissolve the objective world—including me and Susan and Rudran—and perhaps even yourself?" Kumaran asked.

"Yes. If you and Rudran and Susan don't observe me, I will cease to be—cease to be 'Manju,' wife and mother and friend."

"Quantum theory is good for science but not as a model for life," Susan said.

"Hinduism and Buddhism are earlier versions of quantum theory. Abdicate desire, covetousness, etcetera, and you dissolve the self. Nonobserved desire equals nonexistence of self."

"Madness," Susan retorted.

"Yes," said Kumaran. "Quantum madness."

"Okay, okay," Manju said, laughing now. "It doesn't matter. These thoughts occur to me. I am trying to connect quantum theory to karmic theory."

"How will you do that?" Kumaran asked, unwilling to terminate the discussion.

"Well," Manju said, "karma is a theory of causation."

"What is this theory of causation?" Susan asked.

"Everything in the universe has a cause. This includes a human being too. He didn't just happen. He is dependent on a cause."

"How will we know it?" Kumaran asked.

"By the effect. We infer backwards. If these are the effects, this must be the cause."

"Oh," said Susan and Kumaran simultaneously.

Kumaran continued, "If I suffer in this particular way, then it was caused by that particular event."

"Yes. However, unless you look at the effects and understand them, they are meaningless."

Kumaran and Susan asked Manju to expand on this. "The effects become real when they are observed," she said. "Or rather, as they are appreciated and understood."

"This is too much for me," Susan said, and walked out.

"I wonder why she is always playing the innocent. She is trying to impress you, Kum," said Manju, laughing.

Kumaran was not ready to let it go. "If you succeed in connecting quantum theory to karma, let us all know. The whole world is waiting for it."

Manju ignored Kumaran's remark and said, "Let us see a movie."

"What movie?" Susan asked, coming back into the room, eager to participate in this ploy to change the topic. "Let us see the one at the Metro. It's about the scientist who studied gorillas in Africa."

Manju agreed enthusiastically. Her changes from contemplative moods to mundane ones where she became her normally interesting self often came quite abruptly. To Kumaran, these changes did not seem to be emotional ones so much as moments marking the road map of a philosophical quest, and therefore he did not feel compelled to give them any psychological classification.

The movie was a bore, a cold actress portraying a cold woman, with humans in masks impersonating gorillas. Manju, however, was thrilled by it and kept wondering whether animals were subject to the laws of karma. This was a new element in her thinking, the doctrine of action and retribution that was at the heart of Hindu and Buddhist beliefs and that was to come up again and again in the coming weeks.

One day, she sought to explain her own life and that of her father and mother with the help of karmic doctrine. Her father and mother had died in an automobile accident in India after Manju moved to Wisconsin. She had one brother and no sisters and felt connected only to Kumaran and Rudy. She'd had her father's and her own horoscope cast and read by a local astrologer and now produced it as an explanation of their karmic destiny. As reformed Hindus, her family had not believed in or used astrology, and now, she seemed to be rediscovering it for herself.

It was all very disturbing, and Kumaran did not know how to respond to these developments. Manju had been apparently content and confident working at her career, and had seemed satisfied with the domestic arrangements. She and Susan were friendly and comfortable with each other and often went out together, to the movies on a Saturday afternoons or shopping. Into this idyllic arrangement had now entered this confused mysticism, a little Vedanta, a pinch of quantum physics, a dash of sorcery and astrology. It was as though Manju were searching everywhere for closure and had not found anything satisfactory. He was hoping that she would soon abandon this quest and return to her science and mathematics.

A change did come, but it was neither a breakthrough nor closure. She announced one day that she had brought home all her jewels from the bank and that they were in her room. She offered no explanation for this. Her jewels were a large and varied collection that her mother had given her and a few other pieces she had acquired on her own. They were impressive not only in their craftsmanship, but also seemed to embody a rich and varied tradition. In the evening, when the three of them were watching the evening news, Manju began to talk about her mother. Her mother had been one of those women who had abandoned many of the ritualized ways of a subordinated wife, but had nevertheless remained in some aspects a traditional Hindu consort. While not being servile and subservient, neither had she been overly assertive or independent. She seemed to have achieved a delicate balance between the two poles, and her marriage to Manju's father appeared to have been a happy one. Manju now revealed that beneath all that surface calm, her mother had carried a passion, cultivated from childhood, for a distant cousin who lived in the city. They had grown into adolescence together and then he had moved away, not knowing that he had lit a fire that would burn forever in the heart of his young cousin. Long years later, after both had married, she had gone to visit him in the village, and they had gone together secretly to the hill station in Simla for a week spent consummating a long-ago passion. Then they returned to the city and resumed their normal lives, with no one being the wiser. Manju learned of this episode from her mother, who swore that no physical consummation had occurred. They had probably taken long walks in the garden around the guesthouse, shrouded and shawled against the mist and the cold. They had perhaps gazed deeply into each other's eyes and held hands occasionally before returning to Delhi. Manju believed her mother's story without any reservation. Kumaran learned of Manju's mother's sorrow for the first time the day Manju had brought the jewels home from the bank.

"They are my mother's jewels," she said. "I don't have anyone to give them to."

She looked at Kumaran as if it were somehow his fault. He knew he had done nothing to deny her a female heir. The birth of Rudy had been a complicated one, and it was not possible for Manju to have any more children.

"I have no daughters—not even a decent daughter-in-law," she continued. "I am taking the jewels back to Jalandhar. I think I will give them to Mohinder's daughter."

"Mohinder? That cousin your mother eloped to Simla with?"

"She did not elope, Kumar," Manju said in a measured and icy tone. "She merely went away for a holiday."

Susan managed to keep silent during this encounter. Indeed, she managed to disappear into an indifferent silence whenever these serious discussions erupted between Kumaran and Manju.

"In any case," Manju continued, "I am taking the jewels back to India. I think I will go in April."

"In April? That's barely a month away," Kumaran exclaimed. "Have you made any arrangements?"

"I have told my boss. I will call the travel agent tomorrow." Though her remark actually revealed very little, Kumaran did not give much thought to its vagueness.

Life in the household went smoothly after this. Manju made all the arrangements for her travel herself this time, not allowing Kumaran to do anything. She made the reservations, dealt with the bank, and bought the gifts for the innumerable relatives. She seemed to be in a trance, despite all of her productivity. She displayed an energy and an efficiency that he had not noticed before. Finally, the day of her departure arrived.

Kumaran and Susan drove her to the airport, and it was then that he noticed that she was taking more suitcases than necessary. She had to pay a large excess baggage fee but seemed to pay it gladly this time. She bade them a normal farewell and walked into the boarding area, bestowing on them a final reassuring smile.

"See you soon!" Susan called out. "Come back safe."

Manju turned back, waved silently, and disappeared behind the partitions.

Kumaran felt vaguely uneasy on the trip back from the airport, but did not say anything to Susan. It was the large number of suitcases and the quality and style of the last smile and wave that had set off a line of thought in his mind. On returning home, he went to her room, looking for some sign that would throw light on these questions. Everything, however, appeared to be normal. Her room was neat and tidy, as usual, and most of her sarees and shawls were in the closet.

He went to Susan's room and spent his night there rather than in his own. He slept very uneasily, and in the early hours of the morning, half-awake, he suddenly understood. He sat up suddenly in bed, pondered his conclusion for a while, and then went to Manju's room and looked for her banking papers. She had her own checking and savings accounts, but he couldn't find anything. He wandered aimlessly around the house and went through his breakfast and newspapers silently, a firm conviction forming in his mind.

He was waiting for the bank to open so he could call, and he was wondering whether he should tell Susan. He could not contain himself any longer, and with his hand on the phone, he blurted out, "Manju is not coming back."

"No? Oh, my God! How do you know? Did she tell you?"

"She did, in her own way, but I was not listening." He dialled the bank. After he had made his way through the usual preliminaries to identify himself, date of birth, mother's name and address, the clerk finally said, "The account is closed, sir." Kumaran hung up.

"Oh, why did she do this?" Kumaran asked of no one in particular, but Susan responded nevertheless.

"She has been unsettled for a long time, Kum. You must have known it. All that yoga and philosophy were not mere games, you know."

"Unsettled by what? I didn't know she was unsettled. I thought she was on some kind of intellectual quest. Now, it looks like they were symptoms."

"Your problem is that you don't see what is in front of you. You are always looking away."

Kumaran turned towards her with anger in his eyes.

"She was unsettled," Susan reiterated, "disconnected with her life here. She also knew she could not go back to India and resume her life."

"Did she talk about all this to you?"

"Not specifically, but I just sensed it from the general discussion we had."

"And did she tell you that she isn't coming back?"

"No, of course not," said Susan, who was getting angry herself now. "Why would she tell me and not you?"

"Anyway, let us wait and see what she does. She will at least write and let me know what is going on, surely," said Kumaran, trying to keep his voice even.

"Shouldn't you go to India and speak to her?"

"I don't know," Kumaran said, his voice trailing off. "I don't know what I should do. Let us wait awhile and see what we hear from her."

In a week, a letter did arrive, but it contained no significant news. It recounted her arrival, the meetings with relatives and friends, and other trivial matters. No indication of her intention, no suggestion about her plans.

A second letter arrived a month later. This did have significant news. It was mailed from the town of Cherry in Southern India, and it announced that she had joined an ashram and was renouncing her worldly life. She had given her material possessions to her nephew and niece. There was such an air of finality and decisiveness about this announcement that Kumaran decided there was no point in going after her. Perhaps in a few months it would be appropriate to go and see her after giving her time to settle down, and perhaps even reconsider her decision. He called Rudy to tell him the news and discovered that he had received a letter from Manju too.

"I am not surprised," Rudy had said. "She seemed a little strange lately, a bit withdrawn, shall I say? A bit unreal."

"Oh, yeah? A fat lot you know," Kumaran had retorted as he slammed the phone down.

He was determined to see her on his way to Colombo, although she had not encouraged a visit in any of the few letters she had written. He arrived in Madras, through London and Mumbai, and checked into a hotel. The next morning, he tried to catch the train to Cherry, missed it, and then took a bus in the afternoon.

It was very hot in Cherry, and the landscape looked dry and dusty. Nevertheless, a fine breeze was blowing, wafting in a persistent smell of flowers and making the heat somewhat bearable. He could not imagine how a landscape as dry as this could produce such a profusion of blossoms. They were everywhere. Vendors were selling them on the sidewalks and they were used as offerings in temples and as adornments on the hair of the women, though only the young and fertile ones were allowed to wear them. Widows and sannyasins could not qualify. Manju would not be wearing flowers in her hair, and he should not be taking her some either.

The following morning, Kumaran hired a taxi to take him to Manju's place from the inn. The taxi driver seemed to know exactly where to take him when he looked at the address that Kumaran showed him. "Coming from Madras, sir?" he asked.

"Yes, and it was difficult getting here. I waited for the train for a long time in Madras and then was told that there was no train that day and went to the bus station and was told that the bus had just left. I had to wait until the evening for the next bus."

"When you go to a holy place sir," the driver said, "it is good to meet with obstacles. It is auspicious and shows that if you overcome them, you are keen to go."

Oh, no, Kumaran thought, *even the taxi driver here is a philosopher.* "How do you know this?"

"Oh, everyone knows that, sir. It is common knowledge. A pilgrimage always invites difficulties."

"I hope you can take me to the ashram without any difficulty."

"I will try, sir," the driver said as he changed gears.

Had he, in fact, come on a pilgrimage? To Manju, or perhaps to the presiding deity of the city? The taxi driver took him to a small bungalow on a side street, where Manju was waiting for him on the front veranda. He had sent her a telegram from Madras and given her no time to reply and tell him not to come.

She was dressed in a white saree, and her hair, too, seemed to have become a little white. She looked healthy and had an air of contentment, a sense of repose. Yet Kumaran felt compelled to ask, after the preliminary sallies, "Why did you do this? I knew you were somewhat troubled, but I didn't know it was so serious."

Manju looked away from him, seemed about to say something, but changed her mind and looked away.

"Aren't you going to say something?"

She shook her head and said softly, "There is nothing to say. You know everything there is to know."

"Why not? You walk away, abandon your husband, son, and friends, and live in this dump, and you have nothing to say?"

"I was not unhappy, at least not in the usual sense." She looked at Kumaran, a half-smile hovering on her face. "I realized that I had reached the last stage of my life."

"What 'last stage'?"

"The stage of the sannyas," Manju said. "Surely you have heard of the Hindu theory of life's passage?"

"Vaguely. What has that got to do with you? I didn't know it applied to women."

"I have reached the last stage," Manju repeated, ignoring Kumaran's remark. "I have been a child, become a youth, learned the facts of life, become a householder and fulfilled its responsibilities, and I am now ready to renounce life and live as a sannyasini in the forests."

"But you are not living in the forests!" Kumaran exclaimed. "Just a dump."

"I had to make some modifications. Besides, these stages of life were meant only for males. This is one of the few places where women can come and become a sannyasi or, as we say here, a *sadaka*."

"Are you happy here? Content?"

"Happiness is not something that one craves here," Manju replied. "I have peace and tranquillity."

"What do you actually *do* here?"

"I teach mathematics in the school. I meditate with some of the other sadakas, talk, relax—sometimes sing religious songs."

"That's it? Sounds like a dull life to me."

"It is a methodical search for self-realization and self-understanding," Manju said carefully, intent on making Kumaran get a grasp of her thinking.

"And you can reach understanding doing these things?"

"Understanding is a bud that is closed up inside us. Once our mind turns towards God and undertakes various practices, the bud opens, petal by petal, through successive understandings and realizations, to a final flowering," Manju said, obviously quoting someone.

"One does not have to live in an ashram to do this. One can live in New York and seek understanding."

"Yes, I suppose so. I was not seeking a partial renunciation. I realized that I had fulfilled my duties as a householder to you and to Rudran, and this was what I had to do, to live in this ashram."

"I still don't understand it, this renunciation of yours. I believe in living in the real world and facing its difficulties, frustrations, and joys."

"There is no explanation for renouncing the worldly life that would make sense to someone like you, is there? It just happens. The call came, my guru arrived, and that is all. I realized sometime ago that my life in America was over."

"When? When did this realization come to you? Not because of Susan and me, surely?"

"No, it has nothing to do with Susan. I realized the emptiness of my life long before she came to live with us. She is more an effect than a cause."

"When did you decide on this step?" Kumaran asked.

"I don't know exactly when. I was reading some books and taking the classes at the yoga centre and then . . . I really don't know when."

"You really don't know when you decided to leave us?"

"I didn't leave you," she said. "Both of you left me a long time ago. And my name is not Manju anymore. It is Satya. I have no husband, no son, no daughter, no daughter-in-law, no kin."

"It is an ordinary case of depression." Kumaran realized as the words left his lips that it was an inane and tactless remark.

"I have nothing to say to you anymore. Please don't come again."

"Okay, if that's what you want." He got up and walked away. Turning around, he said, "Do write, if we can help in any way . . ."

He found a taxi to take him back to the inn. At least she looked content, and she appeared to have found a sanctuary. He took the bus back to Madras and checked into a hotel. He still felt exasperated by the sense of satisfaction with which Manju talked about her life, but at least he now understood some of her reasons. Her studies in New York in the philosophy of yoga and Hinduism had not been a mere intellectual quest, as he had thought. Those studies had encouraged her to take up this new life after Rudy's last visit home. Yet he knew that the seeds, or was it the buds, must have been lying dormant for awhile before opening slowly into this. She must have decided on this course of action while still in New York.

So Susan had not been the cause of Manju's disenchantment after all, and now Kumaran felt sure that Susan had been an offering, a gift. He recalled one day after he had begun his relationship with Susan. He had been seated on the couch when she came over and started kissing him. He pushed her away, so she said, "Come on, Kum; don't look so worried."

"It is not worry," he had said. "It just isn't proper, seemly. Manju will be here any moment."

"So?" she countered. "Manju knows about your relationship with me."

"How do you know?"

"That would be telling," Susan said, smiling. She had this habit of starting a story and then halting it abruptly, about either important matters or trivial ones. She would say, "You know Sam, my friend who works for Lynch and Sacks? He is in trouble."

Kumaran would be mildly interested; a stockbroker in trouble could only be financial woes. "Is he guilty of insider trading, embezzlement, or what?" Kumaran would ask politely.

But Susan would stop and say, "Maybe I shouldn't tell anyone . . . I only heard some office gossip." Kumaran would then return to his newspapers and never discover what Sam's troubles were.

"Don't be maddening, Susan," Kumaran said. "Why do you think Manju knows about our relationship?"

"Do you think I should betray a confidence?" Susan said, attempting sweetness and a coquetry. This ability to switch roles from hard-headed and cold professional to pert, girlish adolescent was one of Susan's most endearing qualities. She played many roles with great success. This, however, was not one of her successful moments.

"Don't play these games with me now, Susan. I have to know. I am worried about Manju."

"Why are you worried?"

"She appears too calm and contented, no sign of the usual anxiety and tension."

"And that worries you?" Susan said, laughing.

"Don't laugh. Tell me what you know."

"Well, I suppose you have the right to know. How can I put it?"

"Come on, Susan, stop these games now."

Susan still hesitated, and then, noticing the expression on Kumaran's face, continued. "To put it in a nutshell, I am quite sure that Manju wants me to have an affair with you."

Kumaran hadn't quite been able to believe it. "You mean she knows and has decided not to do anything about it?"

"No. She encouraged it. Arranged it, in fact."

Kumaran was stunned. For a wife to tolerate a husband's infidelity is one thing, but to actually encourage it is another thing altogether. Bits and pieces of past events came into his mind. Manju had initially introduced Susan to him at their own house, as a colleague. Susan had then come, off and on, to their house and finally became a regular visitor. Manju would leave them alone together for long periods of time. Kumaran did not know whether to dance with joy or squirm in exasperation at this bit of intelligence that Susan had just disclosed.

"Oh, my God, my God," he kept repeating, as Susan looked at him with a smirk.

She said, "Manju is very modern, and quite liberated."

"Don't be too sure that there is anything modern about this for an Indian. A junior wife is commonplace in many Indian communities."

But it became clear to Kumaran, as the days went by, that Susan was right. She moved in with them soon after the conversation, and the three of them began their novel existence. Manju had no reason, Kumaran thought, for saying that he and Rudy had moved away from her and left her. Rudy, perhaps, had moved away from her, but he had moved away from Kumaran too. They had both lost him. Foreigners to the language of the country—at least to the language of the streets, shops, schoolyards, dance halls, and music centres, even to the religions and attitudes of the times—they had become foreigners to their son too. He had started moving away from them when he finished high school. He had been reluctant to bring his friends, and later, his girlfriends, home. His home seemed strange and outlandish to him. There were odd pictures on the wall and the house smelled weird too. He had now come to be called Rudy, and even before he went away to college in California, both Kumaran and Manju knew that they had lost their Lankan-Panjabi son to America. The manner of his marriage to Carol was merely the last step in a series of events that had begun long ago.

III

PERADENIYA

KUMARAN CAME BACK FROM Lalith's party and went straight to bed. He couldn't, however, go to sleep. His head was streaming with thoughts of Peradeniya, the Peradeniya of his youth, the place where had made lasting friends. Eventually he dozed off. He woke up the next morning and decided to go to Peradeniya that very day. He telephoned Wijaya and told him to make the necessary arrangements for his talk. The trains to the central part of the island left frequently from the main railway station in Colombo. He arrived there in the early afternoon and found himself, once again, lost without the ability to speak or read Sinhalese. He had left Lanka, which had all its directional and traffic signs and guides in English, Sinhalese, and Tamil, two of which he could speak, read, and write, and had arrived to a monolingual system running on the one he could not. He felt excluded from all the local proceedings as he made his way with some difficulty to the train to Peradeniya.

The train pulled out of Colombo and started its journey to the higher elevations of central Lanka. Peradeniya was only halfway up in the mountains, and the journey was one of the most pleasant in the country. The hot and humid climate of Colombo gradually gave way to a cooler atmosphere. The trees and shrubs on the side of the railway track became more lush, green, and wet, and gave the impression, as the train progressed, of a slow, steady regeneration.

The train began to make its slow ascent along the foothills of the central highlands. Kumaran looked at the green fields outside and recalled with pleasure a vision of women coming out in the evenings to bathe at the wells in the fields. Wearing sarongs from the breasts downwards, they draw the water in small buckets attached to ropes and pour it over their heads. Long, unbraided hair joins the cascades of water falling around their shoulders and trickling down their backs as the sarongs, now thoroughly wet, cling to their bodies.

Kumaran eagerly looked out of the window but found no such alluring sight. The fields were empty of human beings except for a few stragglers going home after a day's work. Perhaps, thought Kumaran, it was the wrong time of day, or perhaps there had never been such women taking baths, even in the past, and he had conjured up only an adolescent fantasy. Indeed, many other things in his youthful past were perhaps imagined too. But Sujata was not a fantasy . . . or was she?

Kumaran turned away from the window and noticed the sullen silence in his railway compartment. No one was talking to anyone, and each one stared through the window or straight ahead with a vacant look. Kumaran was not sure whether he should break the mood and venture a remark. The people immediately next to him were a couple, the man dressed in a pair of trousers and a shirt, both of them a little too tight-fitting and somewhat tattered, and the woman wearing a saree in the Kandyan style. Kumaran asked him a question in English, and felt uneasy even as the words left his mouth because he didn't know if he had used the right language.

"What time does the train reach Peradeniya?"

The man looked at him and answered in Sinhalese. He appeared to understand English well enough, Kumaran thought, but apparently preferred to speak in Sinhalese.

The last time he had travelled this route, on his way to the university in Peradeniya, the scene was more lively, and when his fellow passengers found out that he was going to the Vishwa Vidyalaya, as they called the university, they became friendlier and, in an odd way, respectful. In a mixture of Sinhalese and English, they had engaged him in real conversations. This time, however, his urges to socialize were forestalled by the laconic responses and the sullen silence in the compartment. Kumaran turned all his thoughts to the greenery outside—and to Sujata.

ॐ

He had met Sujata within a few weeks of his arrival in Peradeniya. The University had decided to honour Lanka's leading artist with an exhibition, and there she was, standing beside one of his paintings. George Keyt, a descendant of European settlers in the island, had become a notable painter. He had rendered a variety of themes from Hindu and Buddhist mythology into an art that was a unique blending of modern European theories and techniques and Indian themes . . .

Things and beings represented in any true art are never represented as things in themselves. Therefore, it is permissible that, independently of their set incidentalism, light and shadow and perspective and recession of planes may be handled in an arbitrary way.

Kumaran recalled Keyt's words from the catalogue for the exhibition. He was still able to remember them vividly, since he had discussed them later with Sujata. Everything connected with Sujata and Peradeniya, every detail and moment, had remained with him all these years. Light and shadow and perspective and a recession of planes that she was, he could see her any time he wished, standing in front of a work entitled "The Afflicted Woman" and studying it intently. She, however, had not appeared afflicted at all, nor were her light and shadow put together in any arbitrary way. She looked radiant in a pale blue saree over a dark blue blouse. Her outfit was assembled carefully to give an impression of studied elegance. Her hair, done in a long braid, snaked itself along her spine and came to rest on the small of her back. Kumaran recalled that he had suddenly lost interest in Keyt's voluptuous "The Lovers," instead becoming absorbed in the image of Sujata. She became aware of his scrutiny, so she turned to face him and stared right back.

Kumaran realized later that, normally, a Lankan girl would not do a thing like that. Most, if not all, would blush, look away quickly, and walk on. Sujata, however, had looked directly at him, a half-smile on her lips. He should have gone up to her and spoken to her. Kumaran couldn't seem to talk, though. He was the one who blushed, looked away, and walked off, as Sujata was to tell him, again and again, after they had come to know each other well. Kumaran did ask, later, why she had looked back at him that way.

"I was looking at the Keyt painting, and then I looked up, and there you were, gazing at me, and you looked like the parallel to Keyt," she said. "I thought you were a sculpture of the Afflicted Man."

He had become a member of the Art Circle, and the two met again at its meetings. The Art Circle was a small group of students interested in painting and sculpture. They would meet once a month, ostensibly to promote the "study and appreciation of art," according to their leaflet. Initially, the members kept themselves busy studying and discussing the books in the library about European painting, and most of them became quite well informed about the subject. Soon, however, they came to realize that the Art Circle did not really have as much to do with art as it did with clubbing. Kumaran suggested that one way out of this was to organize an exhibition of student work. At that time, the university did not teach art in any shape or form. It was the formative years of the campus, and the study of art was not considered as important as economics or history. Art was strictly an amateur business.

Kumaran's idea of an exhibition of local talent was received with misgivings by the Circle. He was nevertheless commissioned to organize it. He wrote a number of announcements about the exhibition and invited the students to submit their work. No work would be rejected, Kumaran stated in the flyers he designed, knowing well that there might not be enough for an exhibition. He proved to be right. Only four paintings were submitted: one by Sujata, a study in the Keytsian mode of a pair of lovers, and three by a member of the faculty. It was, of course, not possible to mount an exhibition with just four paintings, so the Circle abandoned the idea.

It was at a meeting of the Art Circle after this fiasco that Sujata suggested that they study the arts and crafts of the local villages.

"We are too obsessed with European stuff," she had declared. "It is time to take the local artists seriously."

"What do you mean, 'study'?" Lakshmi had asked.

Sujata had her answer ready. "Why don't we go and visit the villages around here, and talk to the people, and find out how they use their art, how they live with the things, how they make them? You know, Dumbara mats are made in a village near here."

"I think that is a wonderful idea," Vivek agreed. "Quite wonderful, indeed, studying the peoples' art rather than bourgeois art." Vivek had recently become a Marxist and was reading about socialist realism.

Kumaran felt doubtful that anything could come out of this. "I am sure there is people's art," he had said, "but what do we *do* with it? Do we go and look at brassware being cast or the mats being woven and come back feeling good?"

"No," Nalini said. "Let us go and study their techniques, their craft, even the way they learn it and pass it on."

"Yes, that's it," exclaimed Sujata. "We can meet later and discuss it. Maybe even write something for the campus journal."

Sujata's enthusiasm was caught by the others, and the project was launched. They decided that it would be unwise for a whole group to descend on the village of Henawela, a few miles from Peradeniya, to study the people's arts and crafts. They decided it would be better to send just two people to a site and wait for their report. Kumaran and Sujata were chosen, so on the following Saturday, they set off to Henawela on a bus.

Sujata talked freely with the villagers. She would stand and watch the women, totally absorbed, work the simple looms to weave the thin strands of dried straw to produce a mat with delicately coloured bird and animal motifs. Kumaran, too, stood and watched the moves of the weavers for awhile, but he grew tired, so he went out looking for a young coconut to drink. When he came back, he found Sujata sitting on a mat, talking to one of the weavers. The woman was thin and wiry, with slightly protruding teeth, reddish from betel chewing. She would at first answer laconically but then suddenly produce a torrent of conversation. Sujata had already told the villagers that she and Kumaran were interested in learning about the weaving of the mats, and she'd won their trust with her smiling, though somewhat aloof, attitude. No pretence of camaraderie or equality for Sujata; that surely would not have worked. The villagers of lower caste, who did only manual work, would have been impressed only by a certain condescension. Sujata knew this almost instinctively and did not choose any easy egalitarian modes.

Sujata would engage the weavers in conversations and tease out various bits of information about the weaving. She would ask, "When did you start weaving mats?"

The woman would look to her, smile, and say, "I don't remember when I started. As long as I can remember. From my childhood, I think."

Sujata would ask, "Who taught you?"

The weaver would say without hesitation, "My mother. I would sit and watch her and my aunt, who used to live with us, sit here in the same place and work, and I would sit and watch and talk and learn."

Sujata would go on like this, unobtrusively constructing a chain of conversations and eliciting information as she went along. "And the designs, the patterns, how do you know them?" she'd ask.

The woman would say, "I just know them; that is all."

"Do you mind if I sketch you as you weave?"

The woman had no objection, and Kumaran found himself on Saturdays carrying a small easel and other materials to enable Sujata to capture the weaver at work. Sujata was bubbling over with excitement, and Kumaran could understand it. There they were, at last doing something artistic rather than anthropological. Soon, however, misgivings set in. What were they doing, after all? What was the point of sketching these people? It could only enhance Sujata's reputation and do nothing for the art or the artists.

"Well," said Sujata, "I am recording the work of the people. What is wrong about that?"

"We should be recording the work of the artists, not the artists at work," Kumaran said.

"How do we do that? There is really nothing to do. They have lost their relationship with the living tradition."

"Living tradition? What is that?"

"A living tradition is one where there is an organic relationship between the artist and his work and the society. Today, the artists, the weavers, produce something that is too readily acquired by buyers and put to decorative purposes," Sujata replied.

Kumaran laughed. "Oh, where did you read that?"

Sujata blushed. "Nowhere specific."

But Kumaran persisted. "Oh, come on now, where did you get that from?"

Sujata finally conceded that she had been reading the works of one Coomaraswamy, who had written a book on medieval Sinhalese art.

"Have you heard of him?" she asked.

Kumaran said that he had indeed heard of him.

"There was something about him in the papers recently. He lived in Boston, I think," said Sujata.

"Okay," said Kumaran. "Tell me, what did he say?"

"Yes, he lived in Boston, but wrote about Indian art and Sinhalese art."

"So, he has no organic connection to what he was writing about."

"Oh? I suppose so," Sujata replied, somewhat abashed. Sujata would not enlighten Kumaran any further on Coomaraswamy's aesthetic theories, but instead, insisted on discussing how they should proceed with their work. "These artists are dependent exclusively on the tourist industry and on producing decorative motifs for the houses of the rich. Their work is not used in their community, you know. They've become mere commodities."

Kumaran had something else on his mind besides art and wanted to bring it up. He was reluctant to address it directly because it had to do with their relationship. He wanted to find out whether she knew what was happening to them and whether she knew what the people in the campus were saying about them. It was a small, residential, self-contained campus, and everything, so to speak, happened in public. At least, everybody was interested in the happenings on the campus, particularly those of the romantic sort. Romantic couplings were rare, dating was virtually unknown, and most of the students expected only to finish their degrees and eventually have marriages arranged by their parents. Any ongoing relationships, that is, ones that went on for a few weeks, where two people were seen together, became not only a subject for talk, but people took an active and, at times, hostile interest in them. If a man was seen on many occasions with a woman, the news became common knowledge. The man and woman were then subject to jeers, catcalls, and jests from all.

One day, Kumaran returned to his room in the dormitory and found Sujata's name chalked in bold letters across his door. Earlier that week, someone had written her name and an obscenity on one of his letters and displayed it on a rack. These hostile acts, whatever psychological motivation they may have had, were not taken to heart in Peradeniya, and were considered an essential part of life.

Kumaran felt sure that he should let Sujata know that her name was being used in this way. He also knew that the moment he mentioned this, their relationship would change forever. The easy and fluid friendship between them would become defined. It might, more or less clearly, remain merely that . . . or something else. Kumaran had, by now, recognized that his feelings for Sujata were more than mere friendliness, and that she was quickly becoming an obsession. He thought about her all the time, dreamt of her, and carried on imaginary conversations with her when he was alone. He could not, however, find the courage to take his relationship with her to a different level, and he wondered if she would laugh when he told her about the petty harassments he was enduring. He knew he could not bear that. He therefore took the easy way out.

"You know, I will not be able to go to the village next Saturday. I have to play cricket." He played cricket well enough to be on the university team, but had been neglecting it for some time now. Sujata was surprised.

"I don't understand this fascination you have for cricket. It seems rather a silly game to me."

"Cricket is a living art," Kumaran replied.

Sujata caught the allusion to her remark about mat weaving and laughed.

"To understand cricket," Kumaran continued, "one must get beneath the surface."

"And what will I find?"

"Every move in cricket is infused with drama. Every move is a confrontation between the player and the world."

"Oh, no!" Sujata exclaimed. "Where did you read that?"

"I didn't read it anywhere. I just realized it as I played the game."

"It sounds very profound. I never realized that that hitting a ball with a bat could be all that."

Kumaran was not sure whether she was mocking him again. Nevertheless, he plowed on. "It is a methodical and disciplined management of act and emotion, of control and expression."

"I am sure you cribbed that from somewhere," Sujata said.

"No, I did not. One can't play the game without realizing this. And it captures the game neatly, I think."

"Okay, I will come and watch you express and control yourself."

"It's a game against a local school. It will not be much of a match because they are a bunch of school boys," warned Kumaran. "You may be bored."

Sujata remained silent and just looked at him.

"It's not that I don't want you to come. A pure aesthete like you at a game—does not sound right."

"It is alright! I will risk it," she said, and then changed the subject. "Let us go and look at the brassworkers one Saturday. I am tired of these mats." She had discovered that the people in a nearby village made decorative brassware—vases, ornamental plates, and decorative elephants—and she was determined to add this to her repertoire.

On Saturday, he was in the pavilion of the cricket grounds getting ready to go into bat when he saw Sujata and her friend Nalini seated in the front row of the stands. Kumaran was not sure whether he felt pleased or disturbed. He did feel a little nervous, of that he was sure. As he tied his pads, his heart beat faster and his hands were getting wet with sweat. He had never felt this way before a match. He was rather the perfect cricketer—poised, in control of his emotions and attitudes, and ready to take anything that was thrown at him in a cool, calculating way. He pulled out a handkerchief and wiped his hands before putting on his gloves to walk towards the wicket.

Though three wickets had fallen and sixty-two runs had been scored, the ball still had some shine on it and the visiting team's pace bowlers were still at work. Kumaran did all the right things as he got to the wicket. He asked the umpire at the other end to give him the position of the midwicket, marked it with due deliberation, imperiously looked around the field to check the position of the various fielders, and settled down to face the bowler. He knew that the captain of the opposing team had set a trap for him at deep leg, knowing his skill at the hook. The first ball that reached him, in fact, was an invitation to take the hook, and Kumaran leaned back on his right foot and hit the ball into the stands for a six.

His first stroke at university cricket was a sixer! He acknowledged the clapping from the small crowd and settled down to face the next ball. The bowler did not want to risk another hook to the stands and sent down an inswinger. Kumaran decided to cut it late. He didn't quite make it, and the ball took the off stump with it. Out for six, with one majestic stroke and another foolish one. He normally did not go for these spectacular performances; he was usually a steady and calculating player, known for piling up runs for the team and taking his time doing it.

Kumaran walked back to the pavilion, wondering what had happened to him. His nervousness was gone, but it had been replaced by a sense of exhaustion. To have played so rashly at the fastball was so stupid, and so unlike him. Cricket, for Kumaran, was the embodiment of reason, the very apotheosis of a mind's capacity to take a challenge and deal with it in a controlled and systematic way. He knew he had allowed himself to get flustered by Sujata. He knew that he should have been happy to see her come and take an interest in cricket, in his playing, but all he felt was a certain apprehension.

This feeling didn't leave him during the rest of the match. He fielded well enough when it was his team's turn to take the field, and in the second innings, he batted much better. He did not try any spectacular shots. He watched the ball and the bowler more carefully, played the balls down and kept them down, and resisted all temptations to hook and cut late. He scored a respectable thirty-two and was caught behind the stumps by a ball that shot up unexpectedly from a weak spot on the pitch and nicked the edge of his bat.

Kumaran returned to the pavilion in a much better mood. He casually glanced in Sujata's direction, but did not find her. Apparently she had not waited for the second inning. Kumaran's feeling of having accomplished something at the wicket left him and was replaced by a certain dejection. *Why didn't she wait?* He unstrapped his pads and waited for the match to wind itself down to a draw. In these matches, one-day affairs, there was never enough time to take a match to a finish before sundown and stumps were drawn.

He walked back to the dormitory with his teammates and was quiet all the way. He was in no mood to participate in an analysis of the match, and in the midst of his reveries, he found himself being teased by Tissa: "Guess who came to see Kum play today?"

"Yes, I saw her too," put in Anandan. "Imagine! Sujata at a cricket match!"

"Why ever not?" Kumaran asked. "What is wrong with that?"

"She is so artsy-craftsy. I thought that cricket wouldn't be in her line," Tissa said.

Kumaran did not want to take the bait; nevertheless, he muttered, "You don't really know her," and left it at that.

"It's okay, Kum," said Ravindran. "Nothing like a little romance to spice one's life at Peradeniya."

"There is no romance, just a friendship," Kumaran said.

The ambivalence he now felt about Sujata, the apprehension as well as the joy he experienced when he was with her, and the dejection he felt when she left, was only reinforced by Tissa's comments. What was he to do with this budding relationship? It was getting more serious than he had anticipated, and he began to feel that he could not really handle it. He was twenty years old, and after graduation, if he got married to Sujata, he would have to find a job, go looking for a house to live in, and go through the grind of domestic life. The mere thought of life after the romance, the routine of living with the same person and carrying the burden—emotional, financial, and social—of married life threw a gloom over the glow that he felt whenever he thought of Sujata.

He deliberately missed classes for the next two days and kept to his room. The feelings of doubt and apprehension began to diminish after these days of solitude, and he began to feel somewhat more secure about his relationship with Sujata. He began to feel that perhaps he was exaggerating his difficulties a little, that there was nothing to do but immerse himself in the life that was opening up to him. He went to his class the next day, and there was Sujata, saving a seat next to her for him.

"Where have you been the last two days? I heard you were sick, but you don't look sick at all now," she said.

"I sprained my ankle and couldn't walk."

Seeing her brought all Kumaran's romantic feelings to the surface, and any remaining ambivalence evaporated.

"Next Saturday, if you do not have a match, we can go and see the brassworkers," she said as the lecturer walked into the class.

"No, I can't. I have to practice."

The lecturer began to talk about Gerard Manley Hopkins. He was not very good at commenting on the poet or the poems he was expected to teach, but he could recite these poems splendidly. He was born to act, not teach, and the poems became dramatic texts that he performed. Today, he read Hopkins' "Spring and Fall: To a Young Child," and his trick of picking one student in the class and focusing his eyes on him or her as he read the poem was particularly disconcerting to Kumaran today because it was he who was thus addressed. The lecturer declaimed:

No matter, child, the name:

Sorrow's springs are the same.

Nor mouth had, no nor mind expressed

What heart heard of, ghost guessed:

It is the blight man was born for,

It is Margaret you mourn for.

"The leaves are falling in the grove and the times of one's life are passing by quickly," the lecturer continued, "but should one mourn for the fallen leaves of autumn, for the passing years of one's own life, or should one run faster and take all life has to offer joyously?"

Kumaran's feeling of satisfaction at having overcome his ambivalence about the increasing closeness of his relationship to Sujata was not dissipated by the pessimism that the lecture on Hopkins created. Hopkins must have been old and already besotted with religion to have focused Margaret on the stings of life's sorrows and not on its joys, he decided as he walked with Sujata to the cafeteria after the class.

Kumaran and Sujata continued to meet in classes, go to Art Circle meetings, see movies in the city, and study the folk art of the neighbouring villages, but he never felt any need to define his relationship with her in any precise way. Eventually, though, he was compelled to face such a definition, and it came about in an odd way. The romantic anguish of one of his fellow students, Ravindran, had precipitated it. Ravi had been attracted to one of the students in his class, and instead of cultivating a friendship with her, he had written her a letter containing not only statements about his love for her, but also overtly sexual suggestions. With admirable tact and kindness, she had not taken it to the authorities, but had actually replied, stating that her purpose in coming to the campus was to study and that she was already betrothed to someone else. Ravindran was so shaken up by this episode that he began to drink heavily and blurt out the details to all of his companions.

After one such alcoholic bout, he had come back to the dormitory and stood outside Kumaran's room, denouncing him in extremely violent and obscene terms and bringing Sujata's name into his tirades. Kumaran had not been in the room, but he had heard about it later from his neighbour. Why Ravi had taken such a hostile step was a mystery to Kumaran. The event was disturbing, and Kumaran realized that it could get worse. If every unhappy and unstable lover were to take to denouncing those who had successful female friendships in the dormitory, life would become difficult. Yet Kumaran did not know what he should do in the face of this provocation from Ravi. Maniam, his neighbour, urged immediate action. "Go to him, Kum," he said. "Challenge him."

"Challenge him? What do you mean, 'challenge him?' To a fight?"

"Yes, beat him up. You are so much stronger than he, and you know he is really a coward."

"Oh, no, Mani, I haven't fought anyone in my life, not since I stopped fighting with my brother years ago. Besides, what is the point? Ravi is a bit crazy, you know. Thinks he is like one of these heroes in Indian movies where people make too much of love and rejection."

"At least you must report it to the Warden," Maniam replied. "You cannot take these things lying down."

"No, no, I am just going to ignore it. Besides, any notice I take of it will only magnify the embarrassment for Sujata and me."

"Kum, I just don't understand this philosophy you have, this detachment."

"No, it is not detachment. It is calculation."

Maniam shook his head in despair. "I just don't understand your attitude."

Kumaran did not try to explain his moves to Maniam anymore, though he was willing to concede that Maniam might be right about his philosophy. A calculated life, that is, a life advanced by calculation, can be achieved only from a position of detachment.

Kumaran felt obliged to tell Sujata about this event and the other minor instances of her name being scribbled outside his door and on his letters. She had, however, dismissed all of it as inconsequential. In fact, she had laughed aloud and said, "So what? You are not feeling ashamed, are you, at being coupled with me?"

"No, I am not ashamed. I thought you might not like it, not like your reputation being muddied."

"How is my reputation being muddied? To have a male friend is not a crime, is it?"

"Well, if you put it like that . . ." It is that you are so different from me—you are . . ." He could not finish the sentence. Once again, he was thinking of her religion and her ethnicity, of her Buddhism and Sinhalaness. Sujata, however, didn't seem to hear or understand, or did not want to hear or understand. Years later, Kumaran reflected that, no doubt, with her unbounded optimism, she had not thought that these were obstacles to a normal relationship between them.

"This exquisite sensitivity of yours is what I like about you, Kum," she continued. "This capacity to worry about trivialities." Kumaran was not sure whether she was referring to Ravindran as a triviality or if she meant the differences between them, but he did not probe any further. Once again, Kumaran acknowledged that he had not taken the opportunity to define his relationship with Sujata and had left it hanging in midair. Now, though, Kumaran felt she had defined it for herself, in any case, and with some precision.

The episode with Ravindran had nevertheless upset him, along with the other little harassments. He knew he was not alone in having to face these problems. Many people in the dormitory had been visited with such indignities, and others had to face even more serious harassments. It was no doubt one way in which students expressed frustration with all of the differences they had with one another. Ravindran, however, was a very disturbed person and probably needed therapy. He had taken to harassing others in the same manner, and it took the usual course. He would gather some of his buddies, go to the city, drink, wallow in self-pity, and then come back and denounce someone. Once, he made the mistake of standing outside one Vinodan's room and shouting obscenities at him. Vinodan was a well-rounded athlete and a member of the boxing squad. He came out of his room and thrashed Ravindran so severely that he had to be hospitalized. Vinodan had to face a disciplinary committee and was suspended from the campus for two weeks. When he came back, he received an ovation as he entered the dining hall for his triumphal dinner. Ravindran changed drastically after his encounter with Vinodan and became more subdued.

Yet Kumaran felt that these episodes were indicative of the difficulties he knew he would face in his relationship with Sujata in the long run. It was not fair to carry on with her on campus in a carefree way and then abandon her at the end. How was he to handle this ball that had been bowled to him? He had to watch the delivery, study its flight, and bat it with due caution and planning. Yielding to easy temptations of a slow ball might open him to a deceptive break that would take his wicket. He realized that he had to stop the developing relationship with Sujata. He knew he had to talk to her. His feelings for her had become more pronounced and decidedly serious. The mere sight of her in her light blue saree with a dark blue umbrella swinging casually at her side would create an unparalleled joy in him. Her light laughter, her intelligence, her wit—these were irresistible qualities, and he knew that he might never meet the likes of her again in this life. Yet, he also knew that any permanent relationship between them would only lead to pain and suffering. She would have difficulty with her family, perhaps might even be disowned by them, and the two of them would have to face life in the margins of the two ethnic communities, alone, without family, and perhaps on a lower middle class income. Reason, Kumaran decided, dictated a rupture in their friendship.

He didn't know how to do this, what to tell her, or how much to tell her. He vacillated between various methods and did not come to any conclusion. All he could do to steer clear of her was cut his classes and avoid going out of his dormitory and to the campus. She sent a message to him through Vivek, who shared a class with her. He still did not respond, and she finally took the unusual step of telephoning him at the warden's office at the dormitory. Telephones were uncommon in those days, and only in emergencies were students permitted to use them, from one warden's office to another. The call would come in and the warden's secretary had to send an office boy to fetch the called party. Kumaran went to the phone, and Sujata told him that she was going home for a week since her sister was getting married.

"Will you take good notes in the English class for me?" she had asked, and said, "I will see you when I get back."

The week of solitude and contemplation had somehow enabled him to bypass ordinary tactfulness, perhaps even brutalized him. Taking advantage of the fact that this was a conversation in which he did not have to face her eyes, he said, "No, I don't think we should see each other."

Sujata seemed more puzzled than shocked. "What? What are you talking about?"

"I don't think we should see each other too much. We are getting too attached to each other . . ."

She remained silent for a long time, and then, without a word, put the phone down. Kumaran was a bit stunned by his boldness and brutality, but he also realized that something that had to be done had been done. Carefully, he had studied the ball that a mischievous destiny had thrown at him and let it slide by safely declining to take it and hook it flamboyantly for a sixer.

Kumaran was to realize in later years that he may have declined the opportunity for a dangerous and showy move, but the image of Sujata's beauty and grace, the soft muted laughter, the gentle half-smiles, were to haunt him for the rest of his life. The first experience of passion is a searing one, and it brands its image on one's brain. Kumaran realized that not one day had passed, whether he was in love with someone else at the time or not, that he did not think of Sujata.

Destiny has its own revenge when its will is thwarted, Kumaran reflected as the train took him to Peradeniya these many years later. He now fully understood that it was not the ethnic and religious differences alone that had kept him away from Sujata, but his own loss of nerve, an unreadiness, and an uncertainty about himself. If he had accepted the role assigned to him in Peradeniya and married Sujata, perhaps he would have, in the normal course of events, become disenchanted with her eventually, and she with him, and the two of them could now be enjoying the boredom of the later years!

He and Sujata had continued to see each other in classes and corridors, but they would scrupulously avoid any kind of contact. This went on for a few weeks until Kumaran decided to change this charade. He sought her out in their next class, sat next to her, and whispered, "We must talk. Let us go for tea after class."

She turned around and looked at him indifferently, but did not say a word. After class, she walked away, ignoring him completely. Kumaran followed her outside and walked beside her for a while along the corridor. Still she did not say anything.

"Don't be so emotional," he said. "Let us talk."

She turned to him and said between clenched teeth, "I am never emotional, you smug fool. Just leave me alone. You are too silly for me to bother with . . . too, too . . ." She paused, searching for the telling word: "Shallow!"

"Okay, okay, I will leave you alone." And he walked away.

He and Sujata avoided each other after that very scrupulously, though occasionally, in class, he would find himself gazing at her. He'd catch her eyes and look hastily away, and at times, he found her looking at him and then looking away.

It was time for the end of term examinations and everyone was busy preparing. These were important points of transition; one must pass them, of course, but a high grade obtained in the three subjects would entitle one to seek an honours degree and specialize in one area of study. Kumaran had been behind in his work. Cricket, art, and romance were not a good combination for academic success. His tutor, in fact, had warned him in that peculiar manner he had of phrasing his observations as aphorisms. "Casual attendance in class will lead to casualties at exams," he had said. But Kumaran had paid no heed. Now, the examinations were here, and he had to scramble to borrow notes and tutorials to prepare as well as he could. He recalled how Leslie had lent him his notes and tutorials and helped him in many ways to prepare for the examination, and had remarked, almost paternally, "The trouble with you, Kum, is that you love too many things, and too many people love you."

"Whatever can you mean by that, Leslie? Too many things? Too many people?"

"Cricket, tennis, art, local culture . . . Sujata."

"Don't be silly," Kumaran snorted.

"It is not only Sujata," Leslie continued, no doubt becoming more expansive than he had intended. "You are quite a pet in the women's dorm, I hear. It is your cricket, I think, that does it. A cricketer is the equivalent of a medieval knight, you know. A bat for a lance."

"I don't know what you are talking about," Kumaran said, and retreated to his room, barely able to contain the mixture of anger and embarrassment he had felt at this analysis of his life by Leslie.

His father must have gotten wind of Kumaran's frivolous doings at Peradeniya. He had many friends among the faculty. Whether he had heard of Sujata too, Kumaran was not sure. In any case, he had a solution to Kumaran's problems.

One day, in the final week of the term, Kumaran went back to the dormitory and found a letter waiting for him, with important news.

"I have decided to send you to England for your studies," his father had written. "That is, if you have no objections. I am sure a degree from an English university would be very valuable in launching a career. You can first graduate and then qualify for the bar."

This was a pattern of education and social advancement that the rich Lankans of the earlier generations had practiced. They would have their male children tutored locally in the correct subjects to gain admission to either Oxford or Cambridge University, send them to England to be further tutored for the admission examinations, and, once such admission was secured and a degree obtained, the young man was assured of a splendid career in the local civil service or at the bar. Those were the days in which rich young Lankans were made into proper, albeit brown, Englishmen. They would learn not only academic subjects at these universities, but English manners and customs as well. Kumaran knew that such measures were no longer necessary; nowadays, one could become a brown Englishman without having to go to England! Nevertheless, he did not hesitate for a moment in accepting his father's offer. To go abroad, to live in England, to participate in the life of London, perhaps at Oxford or Cambridge, was too attractive a prospect, however enchanting life in Peradeniya may have been.

Kumaran knew he had to talk to Sujata before he left Peradeniya. He could not just leave. On the last day of the term, he went to her dormitory and asked the messenger girl to go up and get Sujata. The messenger came down and said Sujata had already left for the railway station. Kumaran went back to his own dormitory, borrowed a bicycle, and arrived, out of breath from the hard pedalling, just as the train to Colombo was about to leave. He walked onto the platform at the small station and saw her sitting next to the window. As he walked towards her, the train started pulling out, and Sujata looked at him wistfully. He waved frantically as he ran beside her window. The train gathered speed, and Sujata called out, "Come and see me in Colombo!"

Kumaran waved back and stopped running. At least he was able to see her off and receive a smile, a greeting, and an invitation. She, he felt sure, must have heard of his plans to go to London.

In the end, he didn't go and see her in Colombo. While he was in Colombo making preparations for his journey, he kept putting the visit off, saying to himself that he was too busy, that there was no point, and that there was, in fact, no time to see her.

ლ

At this, his most recent arrival at the Peradeniya station, instead of walking through the campus's leafy passageways as he had done last time, Kumaran decided to take a taxi to Professor Wijayaratna's house. Wijaya, as he was usually called, had been junior to him in Peradeniya, and had graduated, obtained a doctorate at Cambridge, and was now head of the department of economics. Kumaran had been in correspondence with him for some time and had written to him about his impending arrival in Lanka. Wijaya had invited him to come and spend a few days in Peradeniya and give a talk to the students and faculty. Kumaran had gladly accepted, and here he was at the old campus again. He had never returned to the campus after that day at the station when he had seen Sujata off and taken the afternoon train to Jaffna.

The first impression he had of Peradeniya this time was that there seemed to be more people about the streets that lined the campus. There was a bustle and a haste about them that he could not remember from the old days. People, he seemed to recall, had strolled, if not exactly in each other's arms, at least with each other, and at a leisurely pace. The dormitories seemed to have a certain crestfallen look about them. They had apparently not been whitewashed for a long time and looked to be in a general state of neglect. Wijaya's house was on a small hill in the middle of the campus. It was a big, somewhat cavernous hotchpotch, with winding staircases and huge rooms. Kumaran was greeted by Wijay's servant boy and was told he had gone to teach and would be back in the afternoon.

He settled down deciding to take a short nap, and soon fell into a deep slumber. He woke up two hours later feeling thoroughly refreshed. The cool mountain air, no doubt rich in oxygen, had soothed him into a fine sleep. He dressed hurriedly, came down, and was told by the servant that his host had gone to play tennis and would be back soon. Kumaran wandered about the house for a while and then went for a walk. Going down the incline from the house, he once again experienced the bracing comfort of the cool climate.

He didn't want to go towards the tennis courts and meet Wijaya and his tennis crowd just yet. He headed toward the river and ambled along its bank. It was full of young people, a few of them courting couples. They appeared to be walking slowly and in a stately fashion, promenading, in fact. Kumaran suddenly remembered that he should not be here, that he was actually in violation of an unwritten rule of the campus that this area was reserved for couples. Feeling like an aging voyeur, he walked toward the Faculty Club. He knew Wijaya would be there drinking his arrack and ginger beer.

The Faculty Club, he remembered, was a place where the teachers at the university came to drink, play table tennis, and generally avoid being observed by students. Kumaran was not sure whether he should intrude here either, into this drunken, private sanctum that the faculty had created for themselves.

He entered the club anyway and found Wijaya with a drink in his hand, surrounded by colleagues. Wijaya hailed him and said, "I was just coming to get you. I hope you had a good nap."

"I have never slept so soundly in an afternoon as I did today," Kumaran replied. "I don't know why."

"It must be the climate and the air. Everyone sleeps well here."

Kumaran was not sure what had made him sleep so well. Perhaps it had been something else. He sat down with the others and braced himself for the introductions. Somar, it turned out, was a lecturer in mathematics, youngish, bald, and addicted to cigars. He was sipping a drink and smoking a short, dark stump of tobacco.

"I know your brother," Somar said. "I was in school with him."

"Really? I went to that same school. I must have known you too."

"I was junior to you and we didn't talk to seniors," Somar said.

It took only a few more exchanges like this before Jayam, a teacher of Sanskrit, was able to say, "I hear you are coming back for good."

Kumaran looked uncomfortable. "I didn't say anything like that. What gave you that impression?"

"No, no," Jayam responded, "I didn't hear it from you. Someone in Colombo told me."

"That's all right, everyone seems to think that we immigrants will come back, sooner or later. The return of the homesick." Kumaran turned to Jayam and said, "I am not sure whether I am coming back, or what I would come back to. This time, I am here on family business, and Wijaya here invited me to come to Peradeniya and give a talk."

"Hello, Kum! Has the native returned or what?" announced Toussaint, who had just joined the group. "Don't expect anyone to understand your talk. They don't know the lingo, old chap; they are ignorant clods, gone completely native." Toussaint was a senior lecturer in English and had not changed with the times, or at least pretended not to have. Toussaint had been an enthusiastic member of the Arts Club who'd obtained a good degree, gone abroad for his graduate studies, and settled into an ordinary campus life as a lecturer in English. He was a homosexual and was rumoured to be making lovers out of his servant boys. In fact, Kumaran had heard that a succession of good-looking, almost demure boys had graced his house on one of the small hills of the campus. In Lanka, such a style of life was accepted with hardly a snicker. Toussaint spoke in clichés, and was perhaps condescending to his colleagues, but was a well-regarded poet. He wrote in English, but on decidedly local themes and in the local dialect. He pulled up a chair and joined the circle.

Kumaran said to him, "I bought a volume of your poetry at the Lake House bookshop last week. I haven't read it yet, though."

"Mere fluff, mere fluff, dear boy. But read them anyway, you will know what is happening in the country."

Somar laughed at this. "Yeah, read a decadent poet to find out what is happening in the country."

"Decadent, decadent," Toussaint said. "You don't know the meaning of the word, dear boy. Stick to numbers." The mathematician was not rebuffed, but he was willing to concede that Toussaint's work was unique compared to other Lankans who wrote in English. It was strictly Lankan, whereas the others were Lankan Brits writing for a generation that was no more.

Kumaran enjoyed this banter. It was mostly good natured and a characteristic feature of campus life as he remembered. Toussaint continued. "I hope you are not thinking of coming back. My boy, there is no return."

"I know, I know," Kumaran said, falling into the repetitive verbal pattern that Toussaint had introduced. He sought to change the topic. "Will the audience for my talk understand English?"

Toussaint's bantering manner quickly fell away. "Kum, as you know, instruction is in the local languages. English is taught as a second language. It is a popular choice and most of our students will understand English. However, they don't speak it very well."

The others around the table confirmed this. As Kumaran walked Wijaya home, both of them slightly drunk, Kumaran felt relieved that his talk would at least not be completely incomprehensible to his audience. He realized that the people he had met at the club were part of a multiethnic group—a mix that would have probably been difficult to assemble in any other place in Lanka. There was the Tamil professor of mathematics, the Sinhalese who professed economics, the Burgher (or should one say Dutch-Lankan) who was teaching English, and Somar, of mixed ethnicity.

જી

Kumaran woke up early the next morning at Wijaya's house in a reflective mood. Coming to Peradeniya had not been merely a visit to a university to give a talk on his specialty. It was more than that, surely, but he was not sure what else it was. The casual comments made by his friends here, the jogging of his memory about events and incidents from the past, the onrush of feeling elicited by buildings or the bend in the road—all were making this an archaeology of one of the most decisive parts of his life, albeit a short one.

On his way back to Colombo, Kumaran thought about his lecture. As expected, it had been a flop as far as most of the audience was concerned. The members of the faculty understood it, Kumaran was sure, but the students had seemed mystified. Under the right circumstances, "Information Technologies and World Markets" was a topic that could light a fire in a dependent country, but these students were not impressed. Although Kumaran lectured in English, the students asked questions in Sinhalese. They were then translated into English by Wijaya, and the answers were given in English.

Wijaya drove him to the railway station and invited him to come and spend a year in Peradeniya. "Take a year off from the UN, man. It would do you a world of good. Get back into the groove, and I am sure we would benefit too."

Kumaran replied with a heartiness that he did not feel. "Yes, yes, I am sure of that! But what good would it do for you? I cannot speak the language, you know. My Tamil is quite rusty, and I don't know the technical terms, and . . ."

"Not to worry. Few of the senior lecturers are good in the vernacular, either. They just bluff their way through."

"I am sure I don't want to be put in a position where the students are more competent than I am."

"But you don't have to teach if you don't want to; just be a resident."

The train rattled on, descending from the hills to the plains of Colombo with considerably greater ease than the reverse journey. It was dark now, and the scenery was no longer visible, so Kumaran looked around the compartment. It was empty but for two young men, apparently students on their way to Colombo. He was about to start a conversation with them, but thought better of it and walked towards the restaurant car. It would have been embarrassing if they did not know English.

Peradeniya was supposed to cheer him up, but it had the opposite effect. He could not decide whether the place itself and its people had always been that tawdry, or that, at least when he had lived there, Peradeniya was pleasant, hopeful, and romantic.

He couldn't stop remembering that long-ago time at the railway station when Sujata had shouted at him from her rail car as it sped away, inviting him to come and see her in Colombo. She had waved at him, and no doubt she knew that he had come to see her off. Or perhaps the invitation had been a mere polite response to his own wave, not be to taken seriously.

❧

He did go to Colombo back then, to obtain his passport and other travel papers, and had every intention of also visiting Sujata. Yet he kept avoiding it, and with good reason, he felt. He kept imagining the conversation that would ensue, had he visited her. Indeed, what could they talk about? She could tease him for misunderstanding her intentions toward him and say that she really had no serious interest in him. That would have been intolerable. Or perhaps, she would pretend nothing important had happened. She'd be cool and detached and wish him all the best in London. That would have been nearly as hard to endure. No, Kumaran decided, there was no point in seeing Sujata.

He was staying in the YMCA hostel at the time and was expecting his father and mother to come and see him off before he left for London. He had booked a passage on a ship and telegraphed his father the date of departure. He was lucky to have obtained this berth. Normally, one would have had to book months ahead. Kumaran was able to take advantage of a cancellation and made ready to leave. He wanted so much to get away from Lanka as soon as possible and also wanted to arrive in London in the summer to get used to the place before the cold weather set in.

He was loath to see any of his university friends during this period. There would have been too many questions that he could not have answered or did not want to answer. He had not been sure whether he should go back to Jaffna first, or just stay in Colombo and hang around for his father and mother to come and see him off. He finally decided to stay in Colombo.

IV

LONDON

He was wandering around Colombo prior to his ship's departure, avoiding his relatives and friends as much as possible, when he ran into Uncle Sithamparam on the steps of the YMCA. He was a relative of Kumaran's mother, a deeply religious man, who was working as an officer in a bank in Colombo. Here he was, shabbily dressed in a bush shirt and slacks that needed pressing. There were streaks of holy ash on his forehead with a sandalwood *tilak* at the centre. He wore these marks of religious affiliation and devotion only in his leisure hours, whereas at work, he tried to appear a neat and unadorned professional. It was as though he had two identities—a holy man and an accountant.

"So, I hear you are going abroad," Sithamparam had said, as they seated themselves in the YMCA cafeteria. "Why are you doing this? Education here is good too."

"Yes, Uncle, education is good here, but I want to see the world."

"Oh, that is it, then. You want to see the world. Your father is rich enough to support you abroad as well as give dowries to his two daughters."

"Yes, I suppose so," Kumaran said, thinking that he was somehow being reprimanded. "I haven't thought about it. It was my father who wanted me to go."

"You must think about these things. You are old enough now. How long will you be gone?"

"Four years."

"I think you should have your horoscope read before you go. It is best to find out what is in store."

"No, no, I do not believe in all that mumbo-jumbo."

"If you don't believe in it, why should you be afraid? Think of it as a game."

"Why bother? If the astrologer predicts disaster, then it may affect my mood, even if I don't believe in it. On the other hand, if he predicts good fortune, I will discount it anyway." Kumaran shrugged and looked away.

"Okay, okay, no astrologer then, though I know a good one."

"Do you know what happened last time I had my horoscope read?"

"No," Sithamparam dutifully asked. "What happened?"

He told Sithamparam the story. An itinerant astrologer had come calling the year he was to go to the university, and his father, ostensibly an unbeliever, had invited him to read Kumaran's horoscope. After several minutes of study, the astrologer looked at Kumaran's palm as well and then began his commentary. He had predicted the conventional good fortune for Kumaran—success at the university, a happy and well-endowed marriage, three children, a long life, and death at age seventy-five. No reading of a horoscope is needed to make that prediction, Kumaran remembered thinking. Then, as if to add some piquancy to this bland dish, the astrologer had added, "Yet something will happen to you early on that will mark your life forever. It is a karmic weight that you will have to bear."

"And what is this terrible thing that's going to happen to me?"
"You will not know it when it is happening, but you will bear its consequences."

"What can we do about it?" his father had asked.

"Ask the God Velan for help. Do *puja* for him."

Kumaran had not been impressed. He soon forgot about it. The day before he was to leave for Peradeniya, his father and mother had taken him to the temple and performed a puja on his behalf.

Sithamparam had been listening intently. "Okay," he said. "I am going to Kathirgamam tomorrow. Why not come with me?"

"Kathirgamam? Tomorrow?" Then it began to dawn on him that the encounter with Sithamparam had not happened by chance at all. The uncle had been sent to meet him and prepare him spiritually for the journey abroad. It must have been his mother's doing.

"Did mother write to you?"

Sithamparam did not answer the question. Instead, he said, "Why don't you come? I have hired a car, and you and I can go and ask Velan's blessings for your journey and studies abroad."

Kumaran was caught in a quandary. No deep religious feeling had ever moved him, and he thought of himself as naturally agnostic. He had not come to agnosticism by study and reflection, but this position was nonetheless very real to him. He did not want to hurt his mother, though. He had nothing to do for the next few days anyway and had never been to Kathirgamam, a shrine to a god noted for his compassion for the lost, the bereaved, and the utterly hopeless, situated deep in the jungle of the southern part of Lanka.

Kumaran looked at Sithamparam and smiled. "Okay, Uncle, let us go to Kathirgamam. I have never been there. This is as good a time as any."

They set out by car with their driver Nathan in the early hours of the morning from Colombo, a coastal town, and stopped for breakfast at a vegetarian restaurant. Over *masala thosai* and *sambar,* Sithamparam was explaining that this being late August, the main festival at Kathirgamam had just ended, and the place would be free of people. "But during the big festival in July, the place is very crowded. People from every religion come, you know, not just Hindus."

"Oh? Why is that? I thought Velan was a Hindu god."

"He is a Hindu god, the second son of Siva, but the temple also attracts Buddhists and Muslims. I have even seen Christians here sometimes. He is a powerful god. He helps everyone, even those who don't fully believe in him."

Kumaran smiled at this and did not say anything.

"You know, you are named after the god of Kathirgamam," said Sithamparam. "How is it that you don't know anything about him?"

Kumaran had known vaguely that his name was that of the god, but so many names in Jaffna were references to one god or another that this did not seem particularly significant.

Back in the car, Kumaran asked politely, "What happens during the big festival?" knowing full well that Sithamparam was bursting to instruct him.

"It begins in mid-July, on the night of the new moon, and goes on for fourteen days, till the day of the full moon."

"What happens during these days?"

"The stories of Velan and his wives are performed in various ways."

"Oh?" Kumaran said, somewhat uneasily. Though he had grown up in a Hindu environment in Jaffna, he did not know these stories and was reluctant to ask Sithamparam now.

"Skanda, or Velan, or Murugan, as we call him in Tamil, is the second son of Siva, the younger brother to Ganesha. He was born in India and he fought the evil Asuras with his lance (Vel) and was married to Indra's daughter Devasena."

"So that is the god of Kathirgamam?"

"No, no," Sithamparam said, irritated at this interruption. "Wait, there is more. You must understand how he came to Lanka. The chief of the wild inhabitants of the island once found a baby girl abandoned in a yam patch and raised her. She grew up to be a beautiful girl, named Valli, and Velan heard about her and came to court her."

"But he already had a wife."

"Yes, yes," Sithamparam said, growing more patient. "That is permitted in our culture. He married Valli and settled down here. That is why the shrine is so powerful. He is still here."

"Powerful? What does he do? Can he cure pestilences, help the poor?"

"No, not in a general way, but he helps people individually, if they ask him in the proper way."

"What is the proper way?"

"You must do penance to ask for a boon, supplicate yourself, undergo austerities. I will tell you what happened once. There was this fellow who murdered someone and was brought to trial. He made a vow to the god at Kathirgamam that if he escaped the noose, he would hang by a hook attached to his back at every festival for seven years." Sithamparam stopped and looked sharply at Kumaran, and then continued. "He did escape the death penalty—he was, in fact, acquitted."

"And did he fulfil his vow?"

"Last year, in July, I was here and I saw him hanging with various hooks attached to his body. He had built a scaffold on the bed of a lorry with iron poles and had hooks driven into his back and thighs, and there he stayed for several hours every day for fourteen days."

"He didn't bleed to death? How come?"

Sithamparam answered in one word: "Bakthi."

The word meant devotion, faith, unquestioning commitment, the very things Kumaran did not have. He did not tell this to Sithamparam. They sat in silence as Nathan expertly manoeuvred the car along the uneven roads. They passed through Horana to Kiriella and eventually stopped at Pelmadulla. From Pelmadulla, it was a long haul, through Hambantota, Koslanda, and along the Kirindi River to Tissamaharama.

Kumaran wondered whether Uncle Sithamparam had ordered the driver to take a circuitous route to the shrine in order to show him the beauty of the island. He looked out of the window and silently took in as much as he could of the countryside. He was struck more by the poetry of these village names than by the greenery, the vegetation, and the people he saw. He had lived in Lanka for nearly twenty years and had never ventured outside Colombo, Jaffna, and Peradeniya. His uncle might be taking him to a shrine in the heart of the island, but Kumaran felt that he was also being presented an opportunity to get to know Lanka before leaving it.

They arrived at Kathirgamam late at night and found refuge in a pilgrim hostel on the outskirts of the temple grounds. There was no electricity, and oil lamps flickered in the darkness. Sithamparam told Kumaran that they must get up at dawn to visit the temple.

"But I don't know what to do there," Kumaran protested.

"Don't worry. I will tell you what to do. You merely have a wish in your heart, and I will have one for you as well."

They got up with the early signs of dawn and went to the river nearby. After having dipped themselves in it, they walked to the main temple. For its reputation as the home of the redeemer of lost causes and powerful interventions in the lives of ordinary mortals, it was a surprisingly small and unimposing structure. There was one longish building, with none of the frontal Masonic adornments and towers that one sees in other temples in the country, an offertory section in front, and a number of smaller houses on the side. The main building was surrounded by a sandy courtyard and kept scrupulously clean, but the air around the temple was acrid and smoky with incense.

Sithamparam had brought seven coconuts and incense. He took one of the coconuts to the front of the temple and dashed it on a special altar stone. He then gave Kumaran one and asked him to do the same, and to use all his strength. He did so, and the coconut broke into several pieces. Sithamparam prostrated himself before the entrance to the temple and stayed that way for a while. Kumaran was not sure whether he was to follow suit. He stood and waited, and taking his cue from some of the others there, he folded his hands above his head and summoned a wish to his heart. It was just a one-word wish, and he was not sure whether it was the right thing to do, but his uncle had assured him that any and all wishes were honoured by this bountiful god. Kumaran merely mouthed the word "success" as he worshipped the god.

His uncle then walked with him to the temple of Ganesha and broke some more coconuts there. "Ganesha is the god of good beginnings," he said. "He will give you victories."

Kumaran did not tell Sithamparam that he had already asked for success, and he repeated the same request to Ganesha. Nothing is lost in asking for a god's help, even if one doesn't quite believe in him, Kumaran decided. After all, according to Uncle Sithamparam, this god blesses even those who don't believe in him.

From here, the main shrine, they went to the temple of Velan's first consort, Devasena, and then to the temple of a saint who had ministered at the main temple years earlier. After this round of worship, Sithamparam decided to walk to another shrine to Ganesha, which was about four miles away near a small rivulet.

They returned from this round of worship to their hostel quite tired, and in Kumaran's case, somewhat exhilarated. The worship and the odour of the incense had not touched him much, but the environs of the last Ganesha temple had moved him. The temple sat in the midst of rich vegetation, tall shady trees, jungle brush, and the sounds of running water. Amidst this pastoral scene, he had seen deer, monkeys, and a herd of elephants moving and grazing, utterly unconcerned by the presence of humans. When Kumaran expressed his surprise, Sithamparam said, "This was how it was in the beginning."

"No doubt," Kumaran replied, not wanting to contradict his uncle. Kumaran knew that these animals were used to these pious humans who never bothered them, yet he was still moved.

They returned to the hostel, and in the evening, made more offerings of coconuts to the temple, along with some sweet dumplings. The priest marked their foreheads with holy powder. They spent one more night there, and once again set out in the early hours of the morning to return to Colombo. Sithamparam pronounced himself satisfied with the pilgrimage and announced that he had asked the god of Kathirgamam for Kumaran's safe return from overseas. Kumaran did not reveal his wish to his uncle, and his uncle didn't ask for it. It was dark when they returned to the YMCA in Colombo, just one day before his departure for London. Sithamparam left him there, saying he would come to see him off.

He found a telegram waiting for him. It was from his father, saying that he and his mother were unable to see him off, as she had come down with the flu. His father at least could have come, Kumaran thought, and then realized that, mother's flu or no flu, he did not want to face the emotional turmoil of seeing his son off to London, perhaps never to see him again.

Sithamparam arrived early in the morning in Nathan's car, loaded Kumaran's several suitcases into it, and then drove him to the jetty and supervised the disposal of the luggage.

"May Velan bless you, my boy," he said, and left.

Kumaran arrived in London in the midst of a rare heat wave. Later it would all come back to him as he inhaled the aroma of stout and tasted its bitter, burnt flavours. All the warnings he had received about a London that was continually wet and cold turned out to be untrue, at least that summer. It was blue skies and clear sunshine for weeks, and Kumaran appeared to be one of the few on the streets and trains who had the right clothes for the weather. All the others, in their woollens and synthetics, shirted, tied and properly jacketed, suffered in the heat while Kumaran walked casually about in cotton slacks and a bush shirt.

Mr. Ratnam, one of his father's friends who had been living in London for a while, had met him at the jetty at Tilbury and taken him to Putney. Mr. Ratnam had come to study engineering about twenty years earlier and then changed his plans and become a teacher of mathematics at a high school. He had obtained some qualifications in engineering at the Brighton Technology Institute but then abandoned engineering because the money he had been getting from Lanka dried up, for some reason. He had tried working part-time and following his courses at the Institute, but gave up after a year and took to teaching in a grammar school.

Ratnam had gone back to Lanka, married, and returned to settle down in London. He had a daughter, who was about sixteen. She was going to a school in the neighbourhood and was hoping to enter the university to study science. His wife was a stout woman in her fifties, and they were keenly hospitable to Kumaran. They gave him a great deal of information and advice on how to live in London and were very solicitous to his every need. Yet, after awhile, Kumaran felt that their advice was essentially negative. It was all oriented towards his not doing one thing or another and about keeping himself aloof and uncontaminated by the corruptions of the city. What about London's opportunities—the theatre, the museums, the great cultural institutions? Apparently, Mr. Ratnam had lived in London for nearly twenty years without letting these features of London affect or move him in any way. Work, copulate, have children, make money, save money, die peacefully—these were the motifs of Mr. Ratnam's life. Kumaran wondered whether he should follow the same prescription. It would certainly lead to a dull life, but might, nevertheless, lead to academic success. Kumaran decided that a judicious mixture of work and play would be his course. Keeping this in mind, he could enjoy London without losing sight of his purpose for being there.

Mr. Ratnam seemed to know all the details about gaining admission to the university, having helped many of the advanced students in his own school. Kumaran had brought his matriculation certificates and diplomas from Lanka, and he was admitted to study economics without any difficulty.

Mr. Ratnam helped him find a room and drove him to his new home. On the way to the room and away from his wife, he unashamedly brought up another matter: "English girls. There are many of them about, not to speak of German, French, and Swedish ones. In Europe, there is a severe demographic imbalance, the war and all that, you know, and visiting students are easy prey for them."

Kumaran looked at him in astonishment and did not say a word.

"You must be careful. Of course, you can't avoid them, but one must be careful. I came here as a bachelor, too, but I didn't get trapped, you see." Mr. Ratnam looked meaningfully at Kumaran.

"Yes, Uncle," Kumaran said, aware he should use the honoured kinship title older friends of the family are given in Lanka.

But he could not understand what he was to be careful about. Did Mr. Ratnam want him to avoid these girls altogether, or just avoid getting entangled with them on a serious basis? When Kumaran started unpacking his suitcases and arranging his things in his new home, he realized with irritation that Mr. Ratnam was establishing himself as his substitute father in London.

He went to the university the next day. He did all the work that was necessary for entry into the classes, paid his fees, and was wandering along the corridors when he ran into two students standing by the lift.

One of them ventured, "New student?" Kumaran answered in the affirmative. They said that they were going to get some lunch and invited him to join them. He learned that they too were reading economics and that Anand was from New Delhi, and the other, Battacharya, was from Calcutta.

"I have never met anyone from Ceylon before," Battacharya said.

"I have met several from Calcutta," Kumaran countered. "In fact, one of my teachers in my university was from Calcutta."

"I am sure he was good," Battacharya said with a laugh.

"Good enough," Kumaran said.

"Excellent," said Battacharya. They walked to a pub close by and ordered sandwiches. While Batty and Anand ordered ale, Kumaran ordered a pint of Guinness.

"Do you have Guinness in Colombo?" Batty asked.

Before he could answer, Anand asked, "Where are you living?"

Kumaran said that he had just moved into a room nearby on Hanover Street.

"That's good, close enough to us."

Batty asked, "What kind of economics are you interested in?"

"Development studies, economic theory."

"Very good. That's the sort of thing we Asians must study."

Anand interjected with some practical advice. "Buy a couple of tweed jackets and woollen slacks, a tie or two and that will get you through winter, spring, and autumn too. Food is no problem. There are many cheap Indian restaurants around here and you will get value for your money. Or you can buy sausages—a wonderful invention, everything nicely tied up in a bundle—and heat them on a hot plate in your room. And girls! They are plentiful, mostly from Europe. They are looking for excitement."

Wanting to display the information that he had learned from Mr. Ratnam, Kumaran said, "And there is a serious demographic imbalance. There are more women in the population than men."

"So that's what it is," Anand said. "In any case, we can go to the English Language Club. The girls there want to learn English and are eager to meet English speakers to practice. What are your plans for Saturday?"

"No plans. Why?"

"Be ready by two," Anand said. "I will come and pick you up."

"At two?"

"Yes, two in the afternoon." He looked at his watch. "I am afraid I must go," he said, and left rather abruptly.

Batty sighed and remarked, "There he goes again." He refused to explain further and changed the subject. "What are you planning to do in London besides studying?"

"I don't know," Kumaran said hesitantly. "I suppose the usual thing—museums, art galleries, theatre."

"Oh," Batty said.

"One must get some relief from the studies, and besides, one must use the great cultural resources of the city to the maximum. I may even take a course in painting at the Slade School."

Batty again said, "Oh," this time with a sneering undertone, it seemed to Kumaran.

"I also want to play cricket," Kumaran said, to show that he was not all artsy-crafty. "Perhaps join the sports club at the Ceylon Student Centre."

"Cricket, art museums," Batty said, and the sneer was now unmistakable. He abruptly changed the subject. "What does your father do? A landowner, no doubt."

"He is a lawyer, a very successful one. He does own a bit of land, but not a *landowner* as such. We don't have the feudal system in Ceylon." Kumaran had discerned where Batty's question was headed.

"But yet, very bourgeois. No harm. My family are also landowners. Very bourgeois," said Batty.

They walked out of the pub and Batty invited Kumaran to his house. Kumaran studied the books on Batty's desk. He found a book about London and picked it up. Batty said, as he handed over a beer to Kumaran, "That book shows a different kind of London life than the one that Anand was describing—different restaurants, different living arrangements."

As Kumaran flipped through the book, Batty continued, "Orwell pretended to be poor and lived in Paris and London as a down-and-out pauper." He paused. "Not something to interest someone who wants to go to art museums and play cricket as opposed to seeing the living museums of the streets."

"What is wrong with that? I used to study folk art in a village in Ceylon," Kumaran said, noting both Batty's verbosity and his talent for putting him on the defensive. "And I played cricket for my school and university. I opened batting, if you know anything about cricket."

"I suggest you read Orwell's *London* and see whether you will really like this city."

"You are in charge of my reading now? What else should I read?"

Batty seemed to have missed Kumaran's sarcasm. He said, "I suggest Engel's *The Condition of the English Working Classes.*" He fetched the book from a shelf and handed it to Kumaran.

Kumaran left Batty's room with two books and a great deal to think about, and also with Batty's sneers about art, painting, and cricket ringing in his ears.

At two on Saturday, Anand picked him up. They took the underground to Lancaster Gate and from there to a flat in the neighbourhood. It turned out to be a party, of sorts, mostly European girls and a number of white, black, and brown boys. He was told this was the English Speaking Club. After having taken some classes at home in English, girls and some boys from Sweden, Germany, and France would come to London for short periods of time to practice their English conversation. This place also turned out to be the centre for meeting people—isolated foreigners seeking to pool and perhaps assuage their loneliness through a language that no one really spoke very well. Anand explained that one selects a likely girl, chats her up, takes her out for dinner, and so on and so forth. Kumaran could see that Anand was busy doing just that with a tall girl with yellow hair. Kumaran, however, could not get the hang of it. Various women would come and speak to him, but Kumaran found himself giving only short, desultory answers. They would give up on him, thinking, perhaps, that his English was not good enough yet. Anand had disappeared with the voluptuous blonde, Inger from Sweden.

Kumaran went home and began reading Orwell's book on living poor in Paris and London. After a short dip into Engel's tome on the English working class in the eighteenth century, he picked up Orwell again and couldn't put it down. He finished it in one sitting, reading late into the night.

He telephoned Batty the next day and told him that he wanted to talk to him about Orwell. They arranged to meet in the evening at the local pub. Even before they were properly seated, Kumaran said, "Do you think conditions like that exist in London now?"

"Of course they do," Batty replied. "Do you think poverty exists only in Calcutta?"

"No. Of course I didn't think that. But such serious problems? Orwell was not really poor. He was educated and was just playing poor."

"Yes, that's true. But the conditions he describes were real, are still true."

"Perhaps we should investigate it ourselves," Kumaran said, not expecting to be taken seriously.

"Really?" Batty was surprised. "Beats art and cricket."

"Perhaps we should do an Orwell," Kumaran said, still playing the game.

Batty, however, had taken up the idea seriously and was taking it somewhat further than Kumaran had intended. "I don't think we can go and live in flophouses and homeless shelters," he said.

"No, too dangerous for Asians. They might kill you in your sleep. Then we should try something else. We could follow his Paris experience and become dishwashers."

"That's a good idea. We can get jobs in a classy restaurant."

"Or in an Indian restaurant. There seem to be so many about. Well, let's talk about it tomorrow," Kumaran said, and went home.

He stopped at an Indian takeout restaurant and bought some curried chicken and rotis. He was eating them in his room when his landlady knocked. She was a rather plump woman in her forties, a widow with two daughters to support. She had an air of sadness and withdrawal about her.

"Oh, you are having dinner, are you? Never mind. You carry on," she said as she sat herself down. "I came to tell you that I can supply dinner and breakfast for an extra charge."

"That's kind of you. I will think about it and let you know."

"Yes, think about it. It will save you a lot of bother on cold days." She look warily at Kumaran's plate, still filled with curried chicken. "It won't be Indian food, of course. Good, wholesome English food."

"That's all right, then. I don't mind English food."

Kumaran was eventually glad he had accepted her offer. It saved him unnecessary labour.

The next day was a Saturday, and Batty arrived at Kumaran's place in the morning and told him that they should start looking for jobs.

"What jobs?" Kumaran was puzzled, not immediately connecting Batty's suggestion to the previous evening's casual conversation.

"For dishwashers."

"Oh. So soon?"

"I know, I know, you don't need the money. You must be getting enough money from home, but this is research."

Kumaran reluctantly agreed, and they set out for an expensive Indian restaurant that Batty had selected, called, naturally, the Taj Palace. Batty said to the headwaiter that he wanted to talk to the manager, and they were taken to his office. After some questions, the manager said that he could employ them as waiters since they spoke English well, but not as dishwashers. Batty, however, insisted that they wanted to be dishwashers, even if the pay was less than that of a waiter.

"I don't understand. Why would you want to be dishwashers? You are well dressed, speak good English." He paused and looked at them again, more closely. "Are you spies for the Council? For the Union?"

"No, nothing like that," Batty said rather hastily.

"Well," the manager said, "I don't trust you. Try some other place," and dismissed them. They left laughing, promising to try another restaurant, only this time taking care to dress poorly and to speak only minimal English.

The project to go slumming soon lost its glamour after Anand pointed out to them that it was not only very hard work, but also that the fumes in the washing tanks could give one respiratory illnesses. Kumaran, however, had been deeply impressed by the books Batty had given him and hungered for more. He was soon devouring works by Marx and Engels and others under Batty's tutelage. He abandoned the idea of playing cricket, but did make it a point to visit museums and art galleries and often took Batty along too.

After a few weeks of living in London, Kumaran had settled into a routine. Then a new development emerged. His landlady, Mrs. Watson, had been giving him his breakfast and dinner, and it was pleasant enough at her home. He sat at the table with her daughters, who were aged ten and twelve, and was beginning to feel thoroughly at home.

He was reading in his room late one night when Mrs. Watson knocked at his door and invited him to join her for a drink. Kumaran was quite surprised at this but joined her in the sitting room. It became clear to Kumaran that it was not just a drink she had in mind. Anand had to travel to international language parties and engage in insincere conversations to find sexual companionship, and here it was being offered to him in his own home. Yet Kumaran hesitated and became withdrawn and cold as Mrs. Watson drank more whiskey and became more and more bold and amorous. She put some records on the player and asked him to dance. After a few turns, she began to kiss him on his cheeks and then on his lips. They sat down on the sofa for awhile and then Mrs. Watson fell asleep, her head on Kumaran's lap.

"Alcohol is not the friend of romance as it is rumoured to be," Kumaran said aloud as he gazed on the prostrate Enid Watson. He delicately arranged her on the sofa and covered her with a blanket. He went back to his room and eventually fell into a troubled sleep.

Kumaran's sexual experience had not been not very wide, but he had not had the troubled life of many of his schoolmates during their adolescence in Ceylon. He studied in an elite school in Colombo, run by the Anglican Church, and boarded in a private home. Some of his schoolmates were fortunate in having complaisant servant maids at home to help them through their early stirrings of sexual energy. There was also a rumour that one of his classmates had an ayah assigned to him as a sexual companion by his parents.

"This will keep him from trouble and will improve his studies," it was claimed they had said. In the house where he was boarded, there was indeed an attractive ayah. He had eyed her lustily for some time, but did not know how to organize a sexual relationship with her. He consulted one of his friends at school, who recommended "creeping." "Just creep into her room after everyone has gone to sleep and lie next to her. She will not object. She is used to it."

One night, Kumaran did just that. Her name was Somawathie, he remembered. She had not objected, but she was quite surprised.

"What now, master?" she whispered in the dark. "Again? You were just here."

It was Kumaran's turn to be surprised. "Just here?" he whispered back. "No."

"Oh," she said. "This is the *young* master."

It took Kumaran a minute to realize that the head of the household, too, had been visiting the ayah since his wife was away. Somawathie was not unwilling to take him on, and this began a period of both sexual fulfilment and instruction for him.

Somawathie left after a year. She had come to work in Colombo in order to gather some money for her dowry, and after collecting her accumulated wages from a generous employer, she went back to her village and was married. Years later, Kumaran wondered why she never got pregnant. Perhaps she had, and that is why she left. Reflecting on it now, he realized how casually these poor and desperate women were exploited by their employees.

Here he was, he thought, in London, and once again, sexually lucky. Should he take advantage of it? Are there any risks? Isn't it about time he took some risks? The next morning, Enid presented herself in the most normal way at breakfast. She gave her children breakfast, saw them off to school, and then passed Kumaran his sausages and toast. Kumaran felt that he had to say something.

"Thanks for the drinks last night. Perhaps we can go out and see a movie tonight."

It was an easy relationship after that. Instead of a movie, they would go drinking in a succession of pubs, he would take her to bed, and that was that. Enid was rather plump and short, and a little reserved and distant—until she'd had a few drinks. She could then become quite voluble and reveal herself as a wounded woman. She was the only child of a plumber in Birmingham, and her mother had died when Enid was in her early teens. She kept house for her father until she was in her late twenties, and was able to get away from her father's house only when he died after a long illness. She married a travelling salesman and moved to London, putting her small inheritance and the money from the sale of her father's house into the one she owned now.

Her husband had died after her two children were born, and she was now raising them by herself. There was always an undercurrent of sadness in her voice whenever she spoke of those years though she couldn't bring herself to call them wasted years, but that is what they were for her. She was trapped in an ambivalence of emotions; she had known it was her duty to take care of him, but she also knew that caring for him prevented her from making a life of her own, for a long time. She was able to meet few men during the years of her father's long illness, and the ones she met were not able to take her seriously because of her responsibilities to her father. The fact that she was rather fat and ungainly did not help.

Once she married and came to London and started to work as a nurse's assistant in the local hospital, life seemed to have taken a turn for the better, but her husband's death changed that. She had become a rather passive woman, given to a stoic acceptance of whatever she faced in the world.

It never occurred to Kumaran that he was doing anything wrong. He realized that the pursuit of sexual adventure in the manner of Anand was beyond his capacities. He had also realized that he could not develop a serious relationship with a woman at this time. Sujata was always going to be there, and between the kisses and the wine with Enid, her shadow was going to fall. It was difficult carrying this emotion around like a lesion in the brain, a deep indentation in his psyche. He had admired Sujata, cherished her, yes, even loved her, but he could do nothing about it.

He had not written to her before he left Colombo, nor had he visited her. He had picked out a postcard at Aden on the way to London, written "Good-bye" on it, and was about to mail it when he realized that was yet another of his brutal and abrupt moves. He threw the card into a rubbish bin. Perhaps the best thing to do was to write her a long letter once he settled in London and give her all the news about life there and about the university.

He was finally able to do this after a few months in London. He was not sure whether his new relationship with Enid had anything to do with it, but he was able to sit down without any anxiety and write a friendly, if noncommittal, letter giving an explanation of why he could not come and see her in Colombo. He was very busy, he said, with passports and financial arrangements, and besides, he lied, his parents were with him and he could not get away. He never received a reply.

He and Anand were vacationing in Wales that first summer when he reached the decision to move out of Enid Watson's house and out of the relationship. It had become too dependable, too much like a family, and a happy family at that. He had continued to pay his rent, and on the surface maintained an appearance of normalcy. Enid's children had accepted him into the household, and he often gave them help with their lessons. His friends never suspected that he was having an affair with his landlady.

He decided to write her a letter from Swansea, and to ask Anand if he would gather his belongings from Enid's house later. It would be clean, neatly cut, without excesses of emotion, no wrenching farewells and no explanations to Anne and Shirley, the children.

He and Anand had come to Swansea to spend a couple of weeks with Anand's cousin, Suresh, who was studying at the Swansea University College. Suresh had wanted to study metallurgy and had decided that Swansea was the right place for it. It was a veritable assemblage of metallurgical activity—copper, iron, zinc, nickel, silver, and gold were handled by the many mills and foundries that straddled the River Tove. Suresh was working towards his master's degree and was expecting to go back and work in his family's mining business. He was a short, stocky young man with wavy black hair and a thin moustache. He appeared to be a serious student and dedicated to his studies.

Suresh escorted them around Swansea, showing them the industrial centres and shipbuilding sites. It was all very impressive. Kumaran, however, grew tired of this and began to fidget and complain.

"Can we go somewhere else?" he asked. "Drive into the country, see something else besides factories?"

"There is an old Norman castle," Suresh said. "I don't know why anyone would want to see that, though."

"Let's go there tomorrow."

"You and Anand can go there tomorrow," Suresh said. "I have some work to do. There is really nothing to see there. Just a lot of stones, bridges, and thick walls."

Kumaran was elated at this turn of events. Since arriving in Swansea, he had finally arrived at a decision, and he wanted to consult Anand about it. He did not want to leave it for a later occasion. He knew if he revealed his secret life to Anand and conveyed his decision to him, it would be sealed in some way.

The next morning, Kumaran and Anand found themselves in the ruined castle. Wandering among the pillars and stones, Anand asked Kumaran, "What is so special about this place? I don't know why you wanted to come here."

"Why? I suddenly realized yesterday that I had to do something, and I wanted to consult you before I lost my inclination."

"You sound serious. Are you going to give up, go back to Colombo?"

"No, nothing like that. Anand, do you know anything about my relationship with Enid?"

Anand was nonplussed. "Who is Enid? Someone at the Language Club?"

"No, no, Anand. Enid is my landlady, and I have been having an affair with her for some time now."

"Sleeping with the landlady? That is rich, Kum, so very conventional. So that's what's been happening. I wondered why you were never enthusiastic about the Club. I thought you were asexual."

"I am not happy with it anymore. It seemed alright at the time."

"Why are you not happy? Don't tell me she is getting serious. She wants marriage? Is that it? That happens often."

"No, no, that is not it. At least she has not mentioned it. The fact is, I am getting used to it. It is too, too, domestic, too tranquil, and I want out. I want to be free again to seek adventures, like you."

"You really want to leave? It looks like a perfect setup to me."

"I can't stand it anymore. Without realizing it, I have become a husband and a father."

"Do you think she will let you go?"

"Let me go? Why ever not? She has no claims on me."

"Don't be too sure. I once heard of a Nigerian student who was sued by his landlady for breach of promise of marriage."

"What happened then? Did she win?"

"No. He was found liable for two years of back rent, though. Do you owe any money to this woman?"

"No, I don't. I always pay my rent. I insisted on it. Besides, she could not afford to live without it."

"You are clean there." Kumaran noticed that Anand was beginning to think like a lawyer. Anand continued, "Better move out, but you must do it gently and slowly."

"How do I do that?"

"I know what you can do. Move into our house. Sundar is leaving at the end of the next term, and you can tell the landlady that you want to live in a house now because you feel crammed in your little room."

"Yes, that is one solution. So can I move into your house?"

"Yes. Next term. You have a little more than a month to prepare her."

They returned from Swansea and Kumaran decided to tell Enid about his intentions. He abandoned the idea of writing a letter and absconding, as it were. It smacked too much of the way he had broken it with Sujata.

The months with Enid had been formative ones for Kumaran. His sexual experience, thought not limited, had been somewhat one-sided before he came to London. He realized that although it was he who had crept into Somawathie's bed and initiated their encounters after that, she was the one in control. He was still a child being taken care of by the ayah, though in rather unusual ways. With Enid, he had experienced an awakening, a feeling that he was now in control. It was true that Enid was older than he was, perhaps by ten years, but the manner in which she let him make the decisions and manage the details of their relationship allowed Kumaran to feel like he was no longer a boy, but an independent young man. He could even face her now and tell her that he was leaving.

It turned out to be surprisingly easy. He broached the subject one morning after the children had gone to school, and she did not even seem surprised. "Will you come and see us again?" she said.

Kumaran noted the use of the plural. "Of course, of course," Kumaran responded, both relieved and exhilarated. She was not going to be difficult after all, and he could still come and see her and the children and perhaps continue to be friends, if not companions—or perhaps even that.

Once Kumaran settled into the house with Anand and Batty, his mother tried to arrange a marriage for him. It was in every way a "splendid alliance," she had written, "and it would give your father and me great joy if you settled down with her." He read the first part of the letter with detachment, not feeling any sense of being pressured, because he did not feel accountable to his parents anymore. They seemed so far away. The sting, however, was at the end of the letter. The young woman he was to marry, or the one his mother wanted him to marry, was living in London and was, in fact, the daughter of Mr. Ratnam, his father's friend who had met him on his arrival in London.

Since the first encounter with Mr. Ratnam, he had seen him and his family very infrequently. On festival days like Deepavali and Pongal, he was sure to be invited, and Kumaran would go and enjoy himself. The traditional food and the sweets that Mr. Ratnam prepared and served made him rather homesick. Yet, but for these occasions, Kumaran avoided the Ratnam family, and they did not pester him. He didn't really want to bother them, and besides, he wanted to live his London life.

"They are a good, respectable family," his mother had written, using the code for caste. "She is Ratnam's only daughter, and you will get a cash dowry in sterling and a house in London. If you approve, we can have the wedding in Colombo this August when you and the girl's party come here."

In spite of the feeling of freedom from parental control that he had felt while reading the letter, the completeness of the arrangements his mother had made and the fact the woman he was to marry was here in London, a telephone call and a train ride away, was a bit unnerving. He could not sleep for days, and he could not understand why he was so completely upset by this development. The woman may well have been attractive, educated, and modernized, and yet he felt he could not consider this proposal seriously. The very idea of marrying Mr. Ratnam's daughter, moving in with them as was the custom in Jaffna, living as an honoured son-in-law, and being held accountable and responsible filled him with panic. *I am not ready for this,* he decided. Late one night, he finally sat down and wrote his mother that he could not even think of marriage at this time because he was determined to dedicate himself to his studies and did not want any distractions, as this was his final year.

He did, however, understand his mother's concerns and anxieties. From the moment the idea of Kumaran's overseas trip was mooted, she had only a single worry—he would marry a foreign girl. She had finally confronted him alone one afternoon, a week or so before his departure to London, and told him, "Don't ruin my declining years by coming back with an English wife."

Kumaran tried to dismiss it with the remark, "What makes you think that one of them would want me?"

"I know, I know. Doctor Sambandan's son married an English girl within a year of his arrival."

"So what's wrong with that? I am sure they are as happy as anyone else."

"But he is not here; he lives there, and his mother does not see her or him or the grandchildren."

"So much the better, Amma. They will not fight then."

His mother ignored this remark and then revealed the wrenching fear in her heart. "I want my grandchildren to look like me or your father, carry our names, be around us, play with us," she had said with tears in her eyes.

Kumaran had nothing to say to this for a while, finally replying, "Don't worry, Amma. I have not decided to marry anyone yet, certainly not an English girl. And if I have a girl child, I promise to give her your name, and if I have a boy child, I will give him Appah's name."

His mother was still worried about his fathering children who would not look like her and who would bear alien names and break the continuity of her line, Kumaran thought. He added a sentence in his letter to her that he was still committed to returning to Lanka single and unattached.

Anand continued his libertine life and somehow managed to pass his examinations. He was too good-looking to be left alone. In fact, he kept up his good looks in many ways. He was always impeccably dressed and carried himself in the style of an Indian aristocrat—erect, head held high, with a slight swagger in his walk. No doubt this caused a great deal of irritation among a number of his fellow students, not to speak of satirical comments. Still, when the news about him came through the aged telephone in their house, it was a shock. Batty charged into Kumaran's room shouting, "Anand is in the hospital, beaten up."

"Beaten up? By whom?"

"Someone at the pub, no doubt. Let's go!"

Kumaran hurriedly put on his jacket. It took them an hour on the underground to reach King's Hospital. When they arrived, they learned that Anand was in surgery and had sustained several head injuries.

Anand died three days later. Batty and Kumaran were able to piece the story together from Ulla, another Swedish girl whom he had taken to the pub, a fellow student from the language lab with whom he'd been friendly for nearly six months. While they were seated at the bar, a group of young men had begun to pass remarks towards them. After awhile, Anand had told Ulla, "Let's get out of here." As they were leaving, they had to pass the rowdy boys, and one of them stuck out his leg and tripped Anand. As Anand staggered to regain his footing, he exclaimed, "You fucking bastard." The boys appeared surprised, looked at each other, and converged on Anand. They knocked him down, kicked him, and stomped on him. One of them reached back, retrieved his beer mug, and emptied it over Anand's now prostrate body and bloodied face.

It was all over in a few minutes, and no one would come to assist Anand. The others in the pub had looked on in stunned silence, and one of them, in the end, called an ambulance. By this time, the assailants had escaped, and when the police came, no one there was able to give a satisfactory description of the culprits.

Anand's body was embalmed and kept ready for this father to come from New Delhi. He arrived the day after Anand's death and made arrangements to take the body back to India for cremation. Kumaran and Batty helped the father to pack all Anand's belongings as the father kept saying, "Wretched country. Oh, why did I send him here?"

Kumaran wanted to interject, "Not wretched country, but wretched rowdies," but kept his mouth shut.

Anand's belongings—his clothes, books, a tennis trophy, and his body—were dispatched to New Delhi by air after Batty had discreetly removed all the albums that contained pictures of Anand with various women.

The final examinations were a few months away, and Kumaran dedicated himself to his studies. He was determined to get a first class score on his examinations, and everything indicated that he might be able to do this. During the previous term, he had become friendly with a visiting professor from the University of Wisconsin, who had encouraged him to apply for post-graduate studies there. Kumaran had followed his advice, taken the necessary admission tests at the US Mission in London, and sent in his application. He soon received word that he had been accepted. He would be a research assistant to a professor and was given a substantial stipend. His father would no longer have to support him.

He had to start his work in the US the first week of September, and he had only a month to spare. He decided to go to Lanka for at least a month and see his family. He arrived in Colombo without telling anyone and then sent a telegram, brief and to the point, to his father in Jaffna.

"Arriving tomorrow, Yarl Devi."

Yarl Devi, "The Maid of Jaffna," was the romantic name that the railway company had given the train from Colombo to Jaffna, the northernmost point of the island. He arrived at the Jaffna station the following morning, and a number of his relatives were there to greet him. He had been away for a little more than four years and had returned with academic honours. It was not easy for his relatives, particularly his father and mother, to hide their elation and pride.

Soon after his arrival, Kumaran announced that he could stay only for a short period of time and had to leave for Wisconsin in three weeks. Despite this announcement, everyone in the family began looking for a suitable bride. His Aunt Raine arrived within three days of his return with a "proposal." The "proposal" consisted of a cheap picture of the intended girl, her horoscope, and a verbal account of her pedigree and the amount of land, cash, and jewellery her father was willing to give as dowry to settle his daughter with a good man. In Raine's eyes, a good man did not mean an emotionally and intellectually compatible person, or even a loving one, but one from a respectable family with a good position in society who showed potential for a steady income. The horoscopes, of course, should be compatible, and the astrologer should proclaim that the intended marriage is in accordance with the stars. His aunt had already seen an astrologer with both horoscopes, and the astrologer said that he was satisfied.

Kumaran was both annoyed and somewhat amused by these moves. "I wrote to Appah even before I came that I did not want to get married now," he protested at the family council that had been summoned after his aunt's arrival and the announcements she had made.

"Most young men say that, but after they see the proposal, they change their minds," Aunt Raine observed.

"What do you mean, 'see the proposal'?" Having asked this question, Kumaran saw that seeing a proposal did not necessarily mean seeing the prospective bride. That came later, almost as an afterthought. Seeing a proposal meant considering the social and financial advantage of the alliance.

"Yes," his aunt said. "Think of the dowry she will be bringing. Her father was an overseer in the government works department, and they are quite respectable people."

His father had not said anything, but his mother made up for his silence. She took up the case that her sister had opened.

"The question is," she said, "why should you *not* get married?"

"Because I haven't finished my studies yet. I want to get my doctorate," Kumaran replied.

His father finally intervened, saying, "And further, he does not want an arranged marriage."

Kumaran felt sure that his father was working on his behalf, though it was not very clear at that moment. His father had never asserted himself openly and tried his best to maintain peaceful relations in the family while performing his leadership role unobtrusively. His interventions in their lives were always subtle and indirect. This was the kind of method he had used to remove Kumaran from his frivolous life at Peradeniya.

"Since he is going to be living in America, the only way he will marry one of our own will be through an arranged marriage," his mother said, addressing his father.

"That may well be true," his father replied, "but you can't force the fellow to marry someone just because you like her, can you?" He tried to convince his wife to leave Kumaran alone. "Let him make up his own mind."

"That's it, then," Kumaran said. "I don't want to get married now."

"I don't know what you are doing to my son," his mother said, turning to his father again. "He will be lost to me, to us, if he goes away now without getting married."

"Leave him alone," his father told her and Aunt Raine. "He can decide for himself; he is an adult now."

Kumaran continued to insist. "No, no, I cannot get married now."

His mother could not be pacified, saying, "At least see the girl! If you don't like her, you need not marry her."

Kumaran, however, felt certain that if he did meet the intended girl, he would be committing himself to the idea of an arranged marriage. He did not want to confront his mother again in this manner, and the idea of "looking over" a prospective bride, only to reject her, seemed utterly unsavoury to him. The cruelty and crudity of this tradition appalled him, yet he knew that most people in Ceylon got married this way. His own sisters would have to face this ritual sooner or later, unless they were lucky enough to attract young men on their own. Typically, the ritual consisted of visiting the young woman's house in the company of one's mother and sisters and sitting down to tea with her relatives. A prospective groom is expected to study the bride throughout these proceedings and then, later on, say whether he likes her to his own folks. If he does like her and wants to marry her, the next day his father goes the bride's place and, as they say, "finalizes" the arrangements.

Kumaran knew that he could not allow the matter to go that far. Yet he felt the power of his mother over him, a hold that made it difficult for him to contradict her again and again to have his own way. Auntie Raine was direct about the meaning of what was happening. She had said, "Sooner, rather than later, one must tie Kumaran up; otherwise, it will be too late."

Tie him, bind him, Kumaran realized, not merely to a woman and the responsibilities and commitments of marriage, but to customs and traditions of his people, and to the land, and the house that the bride would bring with her as dowry. Yet it was not a commercial transaction. It was a way of reintegrating into the community, of planting him firmly in the land and its people.

After his initial intervention, his father withdrew from the proceedings, confident that Kumaran could handle his mother on his own. Kumaran and his mother had to come to their own terms of agreement. Kumaran felt overwhelmed by her dramatic appeals to his sense of loyalty to family, tradition, and country.

He was starting to feel trapped. He told his mother that he could not marry anyone at this time because he was going to America. Now he knew he needed to leave soon.

He told his father and mother that he had to go to Colombo to obtain a visa for his trip to America, and he left quickly, promising to return in a couple of days. He couldn't take all his luggage with him, but he said goodbye to his family with all the formality of a final goodbye, knowing that he would not return to Jaffna. He obtained his visa and his airline tickets, sent a telegram to inform his father that he would be leaving from Colombo for New York, and prepared to leave. His father and mother arrived in

Colombo the next day in time to bid him farewell. They knew he had played a trick on them. His father did not seem to disapprove of Kumaran's move and remained cheerful. His mother, though sullen and withdrawn, had finally understood the depth of his commitment to remain single at this stage in his life. At the airport lounge, as Kumaran was about to leave them, his mother started crying openly.

"I don't know when I will see you again," she kept saying. "Maybe never."

"Don't be silly, mother, I will be back soon."

꙳

It turned out she was right. He never saw her again. A bout with pneumonia took her two years later, and he was left with a feeling of unease about being the source of sorrow for her at the end of her life. She had, however, lived to see Kumaran married, if not to a local girl, at least to a Hindu.

When Kumaran arrived in Madison and was making his way through the crowded bus station, he saw a young man in his late teens holding up a placard with Kumaran's name on it. Kumaran went up to him and introduced himself.

"Welcome to Madison," the young man said. "My name is Jerry, Jerry Hudson." He hefted Kumaran's suitcase. "Let's go!" he added cheerfully.

"Very nice of you to meet me, Jerry. It saves me a lot of trouble."

"The foreign student advisor's office sends someone to meet new arrivals if they let us know in time. How was your journey?"

Kumaran had flown from Colombo with a stopover in Amsterdam, and being unable to afford another plane ticket, he had taken the bus from New York to Madison. "That trip was the most tedious one I have ever taken," said Kumaran. "I will never take such a bus journey again."

Jerry escorted him to a car and loaded his two suitcases into the trunk. "Where do you want to go? My mom said to bring you home tonight to have supper with us, and tomorrow you can go and find a place to stay."

Kumaran felt slightly panicked at this suggestion. Going straight into an American home and staying there for a few days was something he could not handle at this stage. The panic must have shown on his face because Jerry said, "Or you can stay at the Y. They have made a reservation for you."

"Yes, that is the best. I will stay at the Y, but I will come to your house tonight for supper."

Jerry took him to the YMCA and helped him settle in, and picked him up again a few hours later. The Hudsons' house was a small cottage situated amongst a row of nearly identical homes. In front of each cottage was a green lawn so neatly trimmed that, at first, Kumaran thought it was a carpet. Inside the Hudson house, there was an impeccable orderliness, everything in its place and everyone knowing their place in their movements and their conversations. The senior Mr. Hudson, it appeared, was a pilot for an airline and was not home. Mrs. Hudson—Jane, as he was asked to call her—was a pleasant-mannered woman who must have been a great beauty in her youth. Fair-haired and blue-eyed, she was still very attractive. "Call us when you feel lonesome," she had said as he left. "Or when you need some warm socks. And you must come and meet my husband."

They had given him a great deal of advice about living in the US and surviving the Madison winter. "It is not really cold here," Mrs. Hudson said, "if you know how to dress for the winter."

Once, in the course of the conversation, she remarked, "You speak English so well."

Jerry, who had obviously been reading about Ceylon before meeting Kumaran, had interrupted. "Mother, Ceylon was a British colony and they were taught English in school."

"And besides, I've been studying in London for the last four years," Kumaran added. Whenever someone told Kumaran that he spoke English well, he always felt an urge to retort, "So do you." He now explained the British connection to Ceylon and Ceylon's educational system to Mrs. Hudson. Kumaran returned to the YMCA hostel completely charmed by his hostess and overwhelmed by the Hudsons' generosity and kindness.

୧

He had arrived in Madison a week after leaving Colombo and Ceylon. The leaves were changing colour and were taking on gradations of hue that he had never seen before. They had yet to fall to the ground and make way for the hibernation of the winter. Should he mourn for them, like Margaret in the Hopkins poem he had learned long ago in Peradeniya?

He recognized that the Colombo and London phases of his life were over, without any warning as such. Here in Madison, in the US of A, he was to begin a new phase, a renewal, even though it was autumn. The renewal did not come solely in terms of academic success, but also in the shape of Manju and love and the taking of risks and the making of commitments.

V

JAFFNA

KUMARAN DECIDED TO GO to Jaffna the day after giving his talk in Peradeniya. No point in postponing the main purpose of his return to Lanka this time. He would go and finish his duties— his duty to his father's soul, his duty to reconnect it to himself, to the family.

This was the meaning of the rite that he had been asked to perform. His sister Sumi had been gathering information and had told him that these rites were devised when sons lived close to their fathers and were able to fulfil their obligations immediately. Now that the sons were living in faraway places, certain improvisations had to be made.

"As the firstborn, you must light the funeral pyre, perform the *antyeshti*, the ceremony of the last sacrifice, and immerse the ashes in the River Ganges," Sumi had said. "Only then can Appah's soul become connected to us, to you."

"But Shan did all this. If the firstborn is not around, I am sure it is permissible for the other son to perform the rites."

"Yes, that was the correct thing to do. But it is necessary for you to do something too."

"But I don't have to go to India and to the Ganges, do I?"

"No, no, all the waters in the world are connected to the Ganges, all the water is Ganges water," she said grandly. "Under normal circumstances, we would all have come to Jaffna and participated in the ceremony. You know, invited all the relatives, given a feast—but now, with these troubles, it is not possible to travel easily."

"I really don't know how to behave on these occasions, but I suppose I will be able to manage."

"Don't worry, Shan will help you. He knows these matters and will act as priest."

One advantage Kumaran felt he had living abroad was that he didn't have to participate in these rituals. But here he was, about to perform a rite that he did not fully understand or accept. His brother and sisters wanted him to do this, but he himself was not so sure. Yet, without fully realizing it, he too must have wanted to do it, or else he would have said "no" decisively and not even come to Lanka.

He was booked on a sleeperette to Jaffna on the morning train. It was a fairly large reclining seat where one could take a nap. Kumaran looked out the window as the train pulled out of the station and wondered how frequently he had taken this ride. It was the main trunk line between the capital city and the northern city of Jaffna and was certainly the busiest. Someone was always going to Colombo from Jaffna or returning from it. This time, too, the train was crowded, so Kumaran was pleased to have a seat reserved all to himself.

Leslie had driven him to the railway station and installed him in the compartment. He had been Kumaran's closest friend in Peradeniya and had made himself available now to ensure that Kumaran was comfortable in Colombo. Once Leslie learned that Kumaran wanted to go to Jaffna, he offered to have him flown there in a government helicopter. Helicopters were being used by government and military officers to reach the outposts of the country at that time, and for those with influence, it was possible to give lifts to friends or acquaintances. Leslie certainly had influence. Though he was retired now, Leslie had once been a powerful government official. He had sent his car to take Kumaran around, and when Kumaran decided to take the train to Jaffna, Leslie took charge of the expedition. Leslie was now standing outside the window of the train telling Kumaran how stupid it was to go to Jaffna at this time.

"You know, the whole place is in a mess," he said. "There is nothing to eat, no petrol for the cars. You won't even get a taxi to take you home."

"I don't think you understand. I am not going there seeking comfort. I have things to do. I can't put them off anymore."

"Yes, I know, I know. You could wait a year, though, and things are bound to be back to normal by then."

"On the other hand, it could get worse, and I won't be able to go back at all."

Leslie was not impressed. "There will be no problem," he said. "The troubles will be over by then." His tone did not indicate any certainty.

"Do you think the conflict will be over in a year? Return to the old days?"

"I hope so. I think it is possible, if we grant the Tamils the rights and privileges they are entitled to," Leslie said as he wished him good-bye. "Come back safe. Telephone me when you get back."

This conflict was certainly no ordinary one. Here he was, having a Sinhalese friend seeing him off to Jaffna where young

Tamil militants were fighting Sinhalese soldiers, raiding banks, and demolishing government buildings. Such attacks often led to the death of Sinhalese soldiers, and officials and Sinhalese mobs would retaliate by attacking Tamils living in their midst. The mobs would run amok like elephants in must, looting and burning Tamil property and murdering any Tamil they could catch. Yet Kumaran noticed once again that his friends from the old days, before the rift between the Sinhalese and the Tamils, were reluctant to discuss the political situation with him in earnest. Whenever an occasion presented itself, they would let it slide or make mild noncontroversial observations and change the subject. Initially, he'd thought they were merely avoiding arguments, but now he wasn't so sure. Indeed, Kumaran had come to the conclusion that many of his Sinhalese friends had reached an intellectual impasse. They didn't know what to think about the ethnic conflict and were not sure where to stand. They were definitely opposed to the division of the country into two sovereign states, one for the Sinhalese and the other for the Tamils, but they were no longer able to defend their opposition intellectually or emotionally. The recent pogroms against the Tamils were so brutal and violent that no one knew what to think or feel. Leslie, too, displayed a certain political lukewarmness, a loss of nerve, if you will, and seemed to have come to the realization that during the last decade, certain irrevocable political blunders had been made.

At one time, Leslie had been in the thick of those blunders. He himself was a child of privilege and wealth, but he'd decided that "the time had come to liberate the masses of the Lankan people from the economic and social degradation into which the feudal order had confined them," in his own words. For him, helping the masses also meant regenerating their religion, Buddhism, which had been neglected during British rule. Leslie himself had been born into a Christian family, but he'd converted to Buddhism after marrying a Buddhist girl he had met in Peradeniya, and he'd become a zealot of sorts.

Leslie graduated from Peradeniya University and joined the civil service. There, he'd risen rapidly to positions of high office. The nativist polices that the succeeding governments of the country had introduced were implemented by Leslie with great dedication. He was an ardent Marxist on the campus, but had now become a keen Sinhala nationalist. This was a path that Marxists and other socialists were taking during those troubled times.

In time, he became the highest government agent in the southern province. He was popular with the people in the southern province who were predominantly Sinhalese and Buddhist. There were a number of Tamils as well, and they all liked Leslie immensely too. They lived in the heart of the city. When the anti-Tamil pogrom started in Colombo, Leslie had not been too worried about it spreading to his province. It turned out, however, that he had underestimated the virulence of this outbreak, and soon, he had to organize a refugee camp for the Tamils. He converted a big high school into a camp and installed a cordon of police to ensure their security. His home itself was converted into a small refuge for his Tamil friends. He did not think it necessary to put a guard outside his own house, though the usual police officer was there. It was more of an honour guard than protection, though. The police officer was armed with only a small revolver.

One morning, Leslie left home to visit the camp. He wanted to ensure its safety and he also wanted to see that food was being delivered. The superintendent of police who was in charge of the camp was efficient enough, and the camp appeared to be in good order. He was at the camp when he heard of the mishap at his own home. A mob had surrounded his house and protested the presence of Tamils. The police officer was trying to reason with them and disperse them when one member of the crowd stepped forward to protest. The policeman then took out his gun and aimed it at the man. This act apparently enraged the crowd. They rushed the policeman and invaded the house, ransacked it, and set it on fire. His wife had taken their children and their Tamil friends, two couples and four children, and hidden in the bathroom, which was soon engulfed in flames. They had apparently tried to get out, but did not make it to safety. Their charred bodies were discovered later just outside the bathroom.

The pogrom was soon over with nearly a thousand people killed and hundreds of houses and shops burnt out. In Leslie's province, there were only a few lives lost or houses burnt. The effects of the riot, however, were very pronounced on Leslie. He could not understand the violence that had been unleashed on the hapless Tamils that week by his brother-Sinhalese. As a Sinhalese and a new Buddhist, he could not understand the source of these thoughtless moves and countermoves. "How can I be held responsible for this madness in the country?" he asked Kumaran on one of the rare occasions when he permitted himself to discuss the event. "What in Buddhism would encourage, or even permit, such brutality as had been perpetrated in the country? Buddhism is a religion of compassion and renunciation and does not condone violence in any form. 'Overcome anger by peacefulness,' the Buddha said. 'Overcome evil by good. Overcome the mean by generosity, and the man who lies, by truth.'" He was quoting from some text, little realizing that religious ideals in sacred books are rarely put into practice.

For Leslie, the national tragedy became intermingled with his personal one, and he found himself unable to continue his career in government service. He resigned soon after the pogroms and joined a research and policy institute in Colombo.

∽

As Kumaran recalled the sad events in the life of Leslie, his friend, he began to reflect on the journey he was on. The train that had brought him to Colombo and to Peradeniya so often in the past was now viewed as a danger in itself as well as a pathway to danger.

"No one knows what will happen," Leslie told him. "No one is in control anywhere. The trains are attacked—sometimes by political gangs, sometimes by robbers—and no one can tell them apart. In Jaffna itself, no one seems to be in charge. At least, several people are in charge—the rebels, the police, the army, the government—and they are all fighting with each other."

Leslie's warnings notwithstanding, the train reached Polgahawela without incident. It was the main railway junction on this route. For passengers coming south from Jaffna, it was a point of transition to go, as they say, "upcountry." One got off the train and waited for the connection to Kandy. Kumaran had made this same journey often. It was this train that one took to go to the university in Peradeniya. Hundreds of students entrained at points north of Polgahawela and deep in the heart of the Jaffna peninsula and reached it in order to go to the university, all on the same day. These trips were boisterous occasions, often leading to rowdy behaviour and, sometimes, to criminal acts. Still, Kumaran recalled, they were jolly occasions, filled with friendships and alliances newly rejuvenated after the break of the vacations, with a great deal of beer being consumed, something with which most of the students, up to that point, were unfamiliar. At the time,

Kumaran thought they were jolly, but now he realized what an annoyance they must have been to the other passengers.

The last time he was in Jaffna, it had been a joyous time, despite a certain tension in his relationship with his father. His father was alive then, and he had gone to Jaffna to stay for a couple of months. It was the last time he was ever to see his father.

His father, after having given Kumaran his freedom to make up his own mind about so many matters in his life, had found, in the end, that he could not reconcile himself to Kumaran living abroad, marrying outside the community, and not participating in the life of the country.

"So, you don't have any feelings for the lives of our people?" he would say.

Kumaran would reply, "I don't know who my people are. Why should I think that the people of Jaffna are my people any more than the people of New York?"

"I don't understand that, or you. What does that mean? The people here speak your language, practice your religion, and are kin to you."

"No, Appah, I don't speak their language—at least, not very well. I have no religion. We are all strangers here, as well as there."

"There you are again, going philosophical. It is fashionable, but it's still nonsense."

"Why nonsense?"

"We are strangers, but some are less strange to each other than others, and that is all we can expect."

"Okay, okay, I don't think we can resolve this. It is too late for me, anyway. I have a career, a wife, a son, and a home in New York, and there is no returning."

"Yes, yes," his father said bitterly. "You were not here for your mother's funeral, and you will not be here for my funeral either."

Kumaran fell silent at this. It was clear to both his father and himself that Kumaran would not be able to come back to Jaffna in time to perform the last rites if his father died while he was in New York.

"I come regularly to see you. I would rather see you alive," Kumaran had said as he walked away.

He knew even before he arrived that his living overseas would come up, but he had not anticipated that funeral rites and his duties toward his ancestors would also. Since he left home for the first time, though, it was always on his mind. He knew that if his father died, his brother would have to stand in for him and fulfil his responsibilities.

The encounter with his father had unnerved him, and he had felt restless and moody all day. He was not able to sleep at all that night and woke up early to the sounds of numerous birds, chirping and chattering away from the branches of the mango trees. He decided to take a walk through the village. He walked to the market and then took the lane towards the rice fields and retraced the steps he had taken so frequently in his childhood, holding onto his father's hand, sometimes running ahead and annoying him. It had been difficult for little Kumaran to stay on the raised footpaths that bounded the fields, and sometimes he fell into the damp paddy and got wet.

Kumaran walked along these footpaths, alone now, looking at the green rice stalks that were being transplanted by women. Their sarees hitched up and tied to their waist, they were knee-deep in mud and rarely looked up at their surroundings. They were chanting a slow, soft, rhythmic song as they worked in unison. This cadence had remained in his memory all these years, so he stopped to listen.

The chanting of the rice-planters and the orderly pathways on the raised bunds of the paddy fields surrounding the vital greenery of the rice stalks soothed Kumaran greatly as he walked back to his home. He found his old friend Ramachandran waiting for him. The day begins early in Jaffna. People get up just before dawn and seek to finish their chores before noon, before the full heat of the sun hits them in the early afternoon. Rama was there at this time as part of this early morning rush to beat the heat, and greeted him with his usual banter.

"I didn't realize that in America, too, people went out to walk in the early hours," he said, and laughed his uproarious laugh. This was one of his most endearing characteristics, the loud and fluent laughter. When he graduated from the university, he had become a schoolteacher. In fact, he became a teacher in the local school, wrote a number of successful textbooks, and had recently been made the principal of the school.

All this success and prosperity had not changed his genial and informal personality in any way. "I am taking you to a dance recital this evening," he announced. Until that question, however, he had followed the pattern defined by custom: Ask questions about health, wife, children, career, and prosperity of family. Rama had asked the standard questions even though he knew they were difficult ones for Kumaran. The questions were answered, and Rama had ended with the usual homily: "Everything will turn out alright in the end; don't worry. Everything is for the time being."

Though he taught Indian, Lankan, and European history in the local school, his real passion was for music and dance. He was extremely knowledgeable about both and never missed a concert if he could help it.

"Who is dancing?" Kumaran asked. "Is she any good?"

"We have a rare treat this time. Yamuna, the best *Bharata Natyam* dancer in India, is coming to Jaffna. The best rarely come here, you know. There isn't enough money here. This time, though, we have been able to manage it."

Although he'd never seen Yamuna perform, Kumaran had heard of her vaguely. In the circles in which he lived in New York, Indian dance and music were not part of the conversation, and though there were many visiting artists in the city, he had never ventured to see any of them.

"I will call for you at five," Rama said. "It will give us enough time to get there."

"Don't we have to make reservations?"

"No, I have two complimentary tickets. I am a member of the organizing committee."

"How do we get there?"

"I have asked Chinnavan to bring the car around four-thirty," Rama replied.

Yes, Kumaran remembered, *one rents a car for the evening at very reasonable prices.* Kumaran had thought of renting a car in Colombo and bringing it over to Jaffna, but he did not trust himself on the local roads anymore. It was not only that people drove on the left-hand side of the road, but even the unspoken conventions of the road had become strange to him. In practice, the pedestrians did not have the right of way here, and vehicles seemed to have all the rights. The pedestrian ducks and dodges the vehicles as well as he can and goes along his way. All of this proved to be too much of a challenge, so Kumaran abandoned the idea of driving on the local roads. He could have rented a car and hired a chauffeur, but he felt that would have been too ostentatious. He had forgotten that, even for middle-class people, this was standard practice here on occasion.

Rama came for Kumaran at the appointed time and they left for the town hall. His village was about ten miles from the town. Cultural events in the city were usually arranged to begin around six and to go on till ten or so. People here had their meal late at night and went for movies and concerts beforehand.

Rama had obtained the best seats in the house. A team of musicians came onstage and began tuning their instruments. Yamuna the dancer came on stage sparkling with jewellery, ankle bells marking her every step. She was dressed in a golden yellow saree, separated in the middle, taken up between the legs, and tucked in behind at the waist. This served as a loosely fitting pair of trousers, permitting freedom of movement. She was wearing a green blouse, which was set off by the greenish border of the saree. Her hair was arranged on top of her head like a pagoda. Though she had tried hard to present a youthful image and appeared agile and slim, one could see that she was in her early fifties.

Kumaran glanced at the program as she introduced herself and her first item. She seemed eager to add a few sentences about the Bharata Natyam performance and its usual order.

"I will begin with an *Allaripu*," she said. "This is the traditional opening of a performance, after the invocation. The Allaripu literally means 'decorating with flowers.' This item is merely a display of the various elements of the dance."

Then she nodded to the orchestra and did a short invocation to Ganesh, the god of auspicious beginnings. She rendered the Allaripu with a delicacy of touch that nevertheless seemed to possess a rhythmic energy. The hands, fluttering like birds taking wing, and the arms, swaying to and fro, seemed to be speaking to the audience in a strange language.

Kumaran must have looked a little baffled, though, because Rama whispered to him even before the end of the first item that they should retreat to the balcony at the back of the auditorium and watch from there.

"Why?" Kumaran asked, puzzled. "These seats are very nice."

"The balcony is nearly empty, and I can explain the dances to you without disturbing anyone."

Kumaran pondered this for a moment. He really did not want any explanation. He could read and respond to the grace and symmetry of the movements and the sheer eroticism of the whole presentation without benefit of a commentary. Yet he agreed, more to give Rama a chance to display his knowledge and expertise than from a desire to be instructed.

They made their way to the balcony and sat in the front seats. They were able to get a good view of the stage, and as the dancer came forward for the second item, Kumaran could see a certain advantage in this new view. The proscenium seemed to frame her in the centre, and with a dark backdrop, her image was clearer and firmer. Located in the middle of a border and with the delicately varied colours of her costume, the image appeared to resemble those that one finds in Indian miniature paintings.

Yamuna began her second item, called *Jathiswaram*, after a short introduction. Rama was not be to outdone, so he said, "Jathi means time-measures. The music and rhythms are more complicated than in the earlier item. *Swaras* are used to accompany this piece."

"Swaras?"

"Series of notes, musical syllables."

"I don't see much of a difference between this and the Allaripu."

"This item is more studied and complicated than the earlier piece. You know, there is a progression here."

"Oh, like appetizers and soup," Kumaran said, laughing.

Rama continued, without acknowledging Kumaran's remarks. "They prepare the dancer as well as the audience. But watch for the precision of her *adavus*—the movement sequences of coordinated footwork and hand movements. Rama would have continued had someone behind not told him to be quiet. Yamuna was now dancing the piece, and Kumaran noticed how precise and coordinated her movements looked. It was not so much her movements that captivated him, though; the underlying coquetry of her presence and gestures held him somewhat spellbound. Kumaran commented on this and Rama appeared pleased. He said, "Wait til the *varnam* for coquetry."

Yamuna appeared once again on the stage and began to describe the next item. Kumaran realized that though she was robust of figure and rounded in the right places, she had a rather thin voice. She was saying, "The varnam is the main item of the Bharata Natyam recital. In it, all the elements of the dance are combined, and with these elements, it seeks to tell a story. Interspersed with these will be various *vistaras*. These are sub-stories that are selected from Hindu mythology that the dancer uses to expand on the theme of the main story. The varnam I am going to do today is 'Samiyai Vara Cholladi.' In it, a young woman longing for her absent lover is trying to coax her maid to go and find him. The lover is none other than Velan, the god, and the woman is a devotee who is longing for him."

With this, the dancer disappeared once again and the orchestra started playing a theme on its own. Rama could not wait to explain, and Kumaran welcomed his intercession this time because he was quite baffled by the introduction to the varnam. "What is a vistara, again?" Kumaran asked.

Rama beamed happily and began, "It is a development in the ongoing story that the dancer introduces on her own. If the story she is dancing is about Velan, she can do a sub-story about his life or about Siva, his father, while the orchestra and the singer repeat the theme or line."

"As clear as the morning light in Jaffna," Kumaran said, laughing. "I am sure I will never understand the mysteries of the varnam. How did gods get into this? I thought it was about a woman longing for a lover."

"Yes, it is very complicated. It is about longing and passion, yes, but it is also about gods and devotees. There is longing there too."

"Oh?" Kumaran said, suddenly getting a glimpse of the complexity of this dance. But before he could ask any more questions, Yamuna had arrived on the stage. She had changed her costume. It was now a powder blue saree-skirt and light golden blouse separated by a silver waistband. This woman obviously had a fine sense of colour for staging, and as she stood there motionless for a moment, her presence seemed to fill the stage and overflow into the audience.

Then, suddenly, she began to dance. The singer began to recite the story of a young woman telling her maid to go and fetch her lover. She would beg her to go in the strongest possible terms and then, all at once, she'd switch to a more sensuous mode to a describe her lover. Kumaran was entranced. The alternating moods and characters that the dancer depicted, the sudden changes of posture, gesture, expression, and emotion, were startling. Having taken only a slightly clinical interest in the proceedings so far, he now found himself thoroughly engrossed. He could make sense of the lyrics and the subtle interplay between the singer's words and the dancer's face, hands, and feet. The gestures, however, that the dancer used were incomprehensible to him, so he turned to Rama. Rama appeared to be in a trance watching the dancer. He managed to mutter, "Later, I will explain later."

Kumaran looked at the dancer, who was vigorously stamping her feet to a complex beat with the orchestra accompanying her every move. She appeared to think better about going forward with this and began to dance more slowly again. The singer began to sing the opening line of the song, and the dancer started a new routine, with the singer repeating the line. Kumaran could not figure this one out at all. The dancer seemed to be entirely on her own, and the singer was not giving the audience any clue about the interpretation of the gestures.

"I am able to understand only in bits and pieces," he mumbled to Rama. "What is she doing now?"

"She is doing a vistara," Rama whispered, afraid to irritate his neighbours yet again. "She is depicting the time that Uma, Siva's consort, tried to trick him into making love to her, with the help of Madan."

"Oh?" Kumaran whispered. "Who is Madan?"

"Madan, Manmadhan as he is also called, is the god of love,"

Rama whispered back, adding, "I will explain later," and went back to watching the dance.

Kumaran too turned to look at the stage and found Yamuna doing one of those rhythmic pieces again, where her rapid footwork matched quick beats on the drum. Rama said, without being asked, "They are called *theermanams*. They punctuate different parts of the story."

They waited for the next vistara, and Kumaran could not help feeling that he was missing the richest part of the evening's presentation.

Yamuna ended the evening's recital with three short pieces called *Padam*. These were little poetic exercises in mime and gesture that were accompanied by a lyric and contained a short story. The dancer enacted them as they were sung. Kumaran was able to pick up the main line of the story from the lyric and to enjoy this part of the performance more fully.

On the way home, Rama was in a state of ecstasy. "What an artist!" he kept exclaiming. "She is more than fifty and is able to do all this without any seeming effort."

"Tell me about all this eroticism and its religious significance," Kumaran said. "What was going on in the Varnam?"

"There was no eroticism," Rama laughed. "It was all a spiritual exercise."

"Oh, come on. All that sexual longing and messengers and impatience and . . ."

"That was not sexual longing, it was just the longing, loneliness, and separation that we all feel. It is merely being expressed in an erotic language."

"A kind of metaphor?"

"Not a metaphor in a simple sense, no, they are both metaphors. The sexual longing is a metaphor for spiritual isolation, and the spiritual isolation is analogous to sexual frustration."

"These are separate realms, aren't they? I am no philosopher, but . . ."

"This is not philosophy," Rama interrupted him, "this is our everyday lives. We Hindus do not separate these things, at least not until the final renunciation in old age."

Kumaran pondered this for a while. Don't separate things? Then, are the erotic and the sacred not separate phenomena? He continued to be baffled by the theme of this religion and the dance. The more he thought about it, the more he could see the signs of it everywhere around him.

Rama continued his lecture. "The sexual is not considered as either a sin or external to human life or even divine life. In the dance, one can see a man being importuned by a woman. At one level, it is a woman overcome by desire seeking fulfilment. The dancer will use all the gestures of an aroused woman in its portrayal. The woman is also a mere supplicant, like all human beings before God, asking to be returned to him. It is simultaneously erotic and sacred."

Having concluded his declamation, Rama looked at Kumaran in the half-light of the car. Kumaran looked a little bewildered, but there was no doubt that the evening had been a revelation to him.

"I merely came to see a dance, and here I am being told about God and separation," Kumaran said. "And I didn't know how ignorant I was, at least about the dance."

They drove in silence for the rest of the journey home. Kumaran continued to wonder about all the things he had missed while he had lived here, all those years ago. He had focused on academic subjects and spent his leisure time playing cricket and tennis. He had, of course, participated in the religious ceremonies at home on a regular basis, but he had never asked any questions about them.

Rama dropped him off at his house and went home, quite unaware of the turmoil he had caused in Kumaran's mind.

৩

Kumaran roused himself from his recollections of his last visit to Jaffna. Rama had since died and would not be there to greet him this time. He looked around him. The people in his railway car were a mixed lot—young and old, men, women, and children. They didn't seem happy or relaxed about going home and appeared to be apprehensive. The hazards of the journey, including the threat of violence from soldiers and rebels as well as the perilous situation in Jaffna, seemed to be uppermost in their minds. Their worry displayed itself on their drawn faces and their mechanical, lifeless conversations.

Kumaran walked to the restaurant car and returned to his seat with bananas for a snack. His neighbour showed every sign of wanting to engage in a conversation, but Kumaran was in no mood to talk. Kumaran quickly turned to the book he had brought along, but his neighbour was not easily discouraged.

"You must have brought that book from abroad, no?"

Kumaran looked up, rather startled. "Why?" he asked. "Isn't it available here?" It was an ordinary detective story that Kumaran had picked up at the airport bookstore in London.

"No," his neighbour said. "We don't import such books anymore. Your book is new." Having solved the mystery for Kumaran, his neighbour introduced himself. "I am one Mr. Swamy from Nelliady. May I know your name, please?"

Kumaran gave him his name, only to be subjected to further queries. In a matter of minutes, Mr. Swamy had extracted that Kumaran had been living in the States for a long time, that he had a son, and that he was returning home to Navaly for the first time in years.

"Who are your people in Navaly?" Mr. Swamy asked next. Kumaran somehow felt that Swamy was too intrusive and too inquisitive. "We are our own people," he said as he picked up his book again.

Mr. Swamy, however continued the conversation. "I know many people in Navaly. My wife's sister married in Navaly. You know the contractor Ragunathan? His daughter."

"I have not lived in Navaly for a long time. I don't know many people there."

"You are a fortunate man. Everything has gone to ruin in our country. No one respects the customs and traditions of our people anymore. The young boys have gone to ruin, too, as well as the girls. They go about on their own now on bicycles, and some have even joined the rebels—they have no modesty, no style." He looked around suspiciously and said, "Perhaps I shouldn't say these things. I don't care anyway. Both my sons—I sent them away. They are in Germany, Berlin."

"Berlin? What are they doing there?"

"One of them is studying computers, you know. The other fellow, my eldest, is working in a restaurant."

Mr. Swamy did not seem unhappy about having his sons away in Germany. He had a resigned look about him, feeling perhaps that he had saved them from a worse fate.

"That's too bad," Kumaran said, feeling some sympathy for him now. "Do you have other children here?"

"Yes, I have a daughter, a little girl. I don't know what I am going to do when she grows up. Her brothers want her to come to Berlin."

"Perhaps conditions will improve here," Kumaran said, and went back to his book.

The train pulled into Vavuniya, on the border between the land controlled by the rebels and that which was still under government jurisdiction. Several soldiers boarded and ordered all the passengers to get out of the train. Both their uniforms and manner were very professional as they searched the train thoroughly. Some passengers, particularly the young men, were given extra attention. Their suitcases were opened and searched, and some were handled roughly. The entire process was accompanied by rude, heckling comments about terrorists and the territorial integrity of the island. Kumaran knew enough Sinhalese to understand the soldier's conversations, but when he was questioned in Sinhala, he was unable to answer. An English-speaking sergeant was produced to examine his papers.

"Ah, foreign-returned," the sergeant said, not sarcastically, looking at Kumaran's passport. "What for going to Jaffna?"

"Visiting relatives," Kumaran replied.

"Not terrorists?"

"No."

"You give money to terrorists?" the sergeant demanded. He appeared belligerent now. The financial support the expatriate Tamils had been giving the Tamil militants was a major irritant among the locals.

Kumaran decided to announce the real purpose of his visit. "I am going to Jaffna to do the funeral rites for my father."

This seemed to mellow the sergeant a little. He nodded thoughtfully and returned Kumaran's passport. "Okay," he said. "Don't get into trouble."

Perhaps it was his mention of a death, or maybe of the ritual, but Kumaran felt he had overcome a major hurdle. He could have been taken off the train for questioning and held indefinitely in some local jail and he would have had to obtain Leslie's help to get out—if he could have even made a telephone call, that is.

The train started again and the soldiers stayed on board. They had not found anything suspicious, but they were accompanying the passengers anyway. It was not clear to Kumaran whether they were there to protect the passengers or if they were being transported north to join the forces in Jaffna. He settled back in his comfortable seat and wondered how late the train would arrive.

The station in Jaffna was swarming with people, and drivers of the few available taxis were loudly importuning likely customers. Kumaran looked around for his brother. He felt confident that his brother had received his telegram and would surely come to meet him. Kumaran could not locate him, though, so he reluctantly hailed a taxi and told him to take him to Navaly.

As the taxi was about to leave the station, a young man dressed in khaki shorts and a white shirt hailed the cab. The driver stopped at the feet of the youth. The young man looked at Kumaran without rancour, but with some suspicion, and asked the driver where he was going.

"To Navaly," the driver told him.

"I have to go to Manipay. You can drop me off there and then go on to Navaly," the young man said as he slid into the seat next to the driver. There was neither a threat in the voice nor a sense of menace in the bearing of the young man, but Kumaran felt both threatened and menaced. He knew that something was going on here that he could not understand. With no question or protest, the driver of the taxi, who was contracted to Kumaran, was willing to take this young man, barely twenty years old, it seemed, to some other destination.

As the taxi pulled out of the station and drew closer to the centre of the city, Kumaran saw the rubble and stone that that had replaced familiar buildings. At the first intersection, Kumaran felt the absence of the Jaffna Corporation. The Jaffna Corporation had been a fairly modern establishment that dispensed groceries and other items from India and England at reasonable prices. It was now in shambles. A few walls and pillars stood as testimony to its former complexity. On either side of this building, there used to be smaller stores, pharmacies, a hardware store, and a textile shop. They had all been gutted by the bombs of the government forces. The hospital, a central medical institution that brought Western medicine to the people without any charge, was damaged here and there, but it seemed essentially intact.

The young man started talking to Kumaran. "Coming from Colombo, are you, sir?" he asked in Tamil.

Kumaran said yes, noting the proper use of the honoured title, the honorific plural, and the passive voice.

The young man, however, seemed to have made his own observations. He asked next, "America or UK?" It was a short, direct, and unsupported question.

Kumaran said, "America," and wondered how the young man knew that he was returning from abroad.

"What kind of job do you have, sir?" he was asked next. Kumaran knew by now that though this may or may not have been a chance encounter, he was being appraised by one member of the rebel Tamil movement. He gave his answer and waited for the next question. It did not come immediately. The young man asked the driver how crowded the train had been, and then he remained silent for a while.

"Which part of Navaly, sir?" the man shot at him soon.

Kumaran gave him the precise address in Navaly and felt bold in asking in return, "Where are you from?"

The young man smiled and did not reply immediately. Quoting from a Tamil poem, he finally said, "Everywhere is my country, all are my kin."

Kumaran felt a little less threatened after the smile and the quotation, so he pressed for some answers. "Why are you asking me these questions?"

The young man visibly stiffened, looked at Kumaran coldly, and said, "Security. Okay, tell me your name and the names of the people you are going to stay with in Navaly."

Kumaran gave his name and that of his brother.

"Shanmugam?" the young man pondered aloud. "Shanmugam of Navaly? Do you know Rajan, then?"

"Rajan is Shanmugam's son. He is my nephew."

"Oh?" the young man said, a little uncertain now. He did not say anything else, but turned around and looked at Kumaran.

"Do you know Rajan, then?" Kumaran asked.

The young man shook his head affirmatively, but he still did not say anything. He sat silently for a while, and then told the driver to drop him off right there. With a bare nod to Kumaran, he left the car and told the driver to go on.

"I thought he wanted to go to Manipay!" exclaimed Kumaran. "Why did he get off so suddenly?"

"He didn't want to go anywhere," the driver said. "He was just checking up on you."

"Checking up? For what?"

"He knew you were from overseas and a stranger here, and he wanted to find out whether you were dangerous or rich enough to tap for money."

"How did he know that I was a stranger from overseas?"

"There are certain questions we don't ask here anymore. They just seem to know everything."

Kumaran sat silent for a while, puzzled at the turn his arrival in Jaffna had taken. His brother had not come to meet him at the station, and then he had been accosted by one of the militants. In what he hoped was a casual tone, he asked the driver, "Who was the young man? Do you know him?"

"He is one of the boys."

Kumaran nodded knowingly. The term "boys" in Tamil was the word the locals used to describe the militants. It was simultaneously a term of affection, condescension, and pride. Kumaran was aching to ask the next logical question, which was about the support they received from the people, but he did not. He knew he would only receive safe, conventional answers. Kumaran elected to remain silent and looked out the window.

The devastation left by the bombing and burning of the city was behind them now, and the landscape looked more benign. The fences that surrounded each house and the greenery, carefully planted to shade the house and its immediate environs from the intense heat of the sun, seemed tranquil enough. Yet Kumaran knew that these houses and the compounds around them were the forts and armouries of the guerrilla movement. Hidden behind these fences, the "boys" would mount attacks on government forces and then retreat into the sanctuary of the houses, which were filled with civilians.

His own house in Navaly, or rather, his brother's house now, and his father's house and his father's house before him, was a benign place in his memory. He and his siblings had all grown to adulthood there, and probably all of them had a special feeling for the place. Somehow, though, Kumaran felt that he valued it more. He had never lived in it continuously as a child, having had to go to Colombo to study at an early age and then to the University in Peradeniya and then to London, Madison, and New York. Whenever he returned to this house in Navaly from Colombo, Peradeniya, or London, he had the feeling that he was returning, not only to receive the love and affection of his father and mother, but also to the embrace of this house.

The taxi deposited him at the front gate. Kumaran affectionately looked at the house through the rich surrounding foliage. It was there, all right, and looked the same as it did in the past. It seemed unnaturally quiet, though. He could not hear the sound of the ubiquitous radio, no conversation or laughter, none of the morning noises of the household.

He paid off his taxi, collected his bags, and walked to the front veranda. His sister-in-law was the first to see him from the inside, and the moment she did, she started wailing. Kumaran knew at once that someone had died in the family. His brother appeared soon and amidst the tears, told him that Rajan had been killed a few days earlier. Now Kumaran understood the reactions of the young militant in the taxi.

"How?" he asked.

"Well, it is a long story," Shanmugam said. "We never wrote to you to tell you that he'd joined one of the militant groups, did we? He had been in it for awhile now. Last week he was killed."

"Oh, no! By whom? Who killed him?"

"We don't know. It could have been the army, it could have been a rival militant gang. We will never know."

Though the Tamil militants were fighting for the same cause, they were split into many warring factions, and their struggle against each other was often as ferocious as the one against the government.

"They continue to kill each other, do they?" Kumaran asked.

"These boys have killed more of our people than the army ever did," his sister-in-law, Sundari, broke in bitterly. "They kill them, cremate them where they are fallen, and then leave."

"We thought this might happen," Shanmugam said, and repeated his earlier angry words. "He could have died at the hands of the army, or he could have been finished off by a rival group or even by his own group. We will never know."

"I am sure his own people killed him," Sundari said. "He told me the last time he was here that he wanted to leave the movement. They don't allow that, you know."

Shan, however, was not sure who killed his son. "We will never know for sure. There is so much confusion around here now."

Shan took Kumaran to his room and told him that their neighbour would give him his breakfast. Once a death occurs in a household, the hearth is not lit until the funeral ceremonies are over, so the neighbours take turns providing food. The kin of the dead are not allowed to go out of the house or even to take a bath until the funeral. Even though there was not going to be a funeral, Shan and Sundari had decided to observe the customs for three days.

Kumaran felt completely out of place in this house of sorrow. After the initial wailing, his brother and sister-in-law, Sundari, did not display any deep sense of loss or grief. They seemed to possess a stoic acceptance of their son's death because they'd been expecting it for a long time. Their son had been dead to them since he'd joined the movement and come home with an AK-47 rifle and ammunition in his belt.

They hadn't expected their son to die in such an impersonal manner, though, and this made them sad. Rajan went to his camp one day, as was his habit, and told his parents not to expect him back soon. This was his usual manner of operation. He would disappear for weeks and then nonchalantly return home and resume his life for a short while, only to leave again. This time, instead of Rajan's return, they were delivered a handwritten note by a courier. The courier came early in the morning while Shan was watering his flower garden. Shan could not help noticing the attitude of deference, almost of obsequiousness, in the courier. This young boy, who could very well have been a carefree playmate of his son in a different time, was now bringing the official news of his death. The note was terse and pointed: "Your son died on the 12th of August at 5.30 a.m." Shan read it and took it inside to show his wife.

His wife did not set up the howl that accompanies the announcement of the death of a loved one in Jaffna. Typically, the women of the household will howl ritually and the neighbouring women will hasten to the house of mourning and join in these rites. Others in the neighbourhood will hear this collective wailing and come to make inquiries and join in organizing the funeral. Sundari and Shan had been the only ones in the house, and it had seemed pointless to wail.

A few neighbouring women came to make perfunctory inquiries and to express their sorrow, but they left quickly. They did not want the boys to know that they were taking sides in the internecine quarrels. It appeared that these kinds of deaths were allowed to fade away into nothingness.

"What does one do," Shan asked, "when one's only son has been killed and there is no body for a funeral?"

Kumaran did not know how to console his brother. Without a body, there is no occasion for mourning or the sharing of grief with relatives and friends, and the loss is made more unbearable. Yet, ruthless and violent as these militants may have been, they at least were ritually thoughtful—they furnished the time and date of the death, so even if a funeral could not be held, other rites could be performed. Since Rajan was killed a day before Kumaran had arrived, they could perform his <u>antyeshti,</u> the last rites, the very next day. For Shan and Sundari, there were no ashes to mix with the sacred confluences of the waters at Keerimalai. They had only a note from his former companions.

Kumaran decided to take charge of the situation. He suggested that they have a ceremony anyway and immerse the ashes of their father that Shan had kept for him. They consulted a priest, and he said that he could not see why they couldn't have a joint ceremony. Even though the priest said the grandfather's ashes could not stand in for his grandson, he was ready with an improvisation. He said that he would write the name of the boy, his asterism, and other astrological data on a sacred betel leaf, and this could substitute for the ashes.

Kumaran and Shanmugam took the imprinted leaf and the ashes and drove to Keerimalai. Kumaran gathered the brass pot that held his father's ashes, crushed the sacred betel leaf and put it into the pot, placed the pot on his head, and walked to the edge of the sea. He then emptied the ashes into the waters. He was horrified to discover that along with the ashes, a piece of a bone fell out. He identified this piece as part of a shoulder joint. It sank into the waters, and fragments of the leaf floated away on a wave. The bone came back with the wave, and then floated back to the sea and disappeared as he Shan and Sundari watched.

After doing a puja at a nearby temple, they returned home and decided to pretend that life had returned to normal. Despite his agnosticism and indifference to rituals, Kumaran felt great comfort in having participated in this ritual for his father and for his nephew. The ritual for the father was over, but what about the son, his brother's son? His father would do the anniversary ritual for him next year, and when he died, there would be no one to do the rites for him. Amidst the sorrow and loss, Kumaran realized that the land he had inherited from his father was now without a proper heir. The line from his male ancestors had come to a stop. Kumaran told his brother to draw up the papers to donate the land to Jana, his sister Devi's son. Kumaran had no use for it now and neither did Shanmugam.

Kumaran returned to Colombo and checked into a small hotel. He wanted to be alone for a while, away from the attention and solicitation of his sisters. He also wanted to be alone so he could meet people without being noticed by his family. He was still not sure whether he should still seek out Sujata. In his earlier trips to Lanka, he had not sought her out, as she was married, and he felt a certain queasiness about intruding into her life. She was alone now, and though he was not quite alone and had Susan to consider, he was open to the possibilities of recapturing something he had lost long ago, some of the feelings, at least a little of the passion. The next day, he telephoned the offices of Radio Sri Lanka and asked for Sujata. After a great deal of confusion at the switchboard, he managed to reach her office.

"Gone out sir," her secretary said.

"When will she be back? This afternoon?"

"No, no, sir, gone to Bangkok. UN work."

Kumaran thought that was that. He was not destined to see her this time either, or perhaps ever. There was no point going to Bangkok looking for her. She might even have gone to Bangkok to avoid him, escape him, after having learnt that he was back. In any case, he really did not expect a reunion with Sujata. And what could he tell her anyway? Could he say that he had been faithful to her, in his way? She was no doubt fat and greying and would not be wearing a blue saree or swinging a dark blue umbrella beside her as she walked. She was merely a symbol now of his youth, of his youthful folly, or wisdom, as the case might be, and of the land he had abandoned. Even if he had seen her, they would have had a desultory, inconclusive conversation and gone their separate ways. Suddenly, he understood the full force of the astrologer's prediction made so long ago on the eve of his departure to Peradeniya. "Something will happen to you," he had said, "something from which you will never recover." It was no doubt a vague and conventional comment designed to introduce a little mystery into the reading of any horoscope and suggest a mystery in the life of the subject. Yet Kumaran recognized the aptness of the comment. It had happened to him, and it happened a long time ago, and he was destined to remember it in all its details.

The events in Jaffna, his nephew's death, his father's anniversary service, had deepened the sense of insubstantiality and disconnection he had felt since he had arrived in Lanka. True, his sisters, his brother, nephew, niece, aunts, cousins, and friends were unreserved in their acceptance and eager to reintegrate him into their community. It was nevertheless time to leave, he decided, and he sent Susan a telegram asking her to cancel her trip to Colombo, but to meet him in London. She had now become the solid connection to the world, his world, that was now located in the US. It was not a grand passion that he needed, nor a revival of a passion for his home, homeland, or for his primal sweetheart, but a calming influence.

The same party that had come to greet him when he arrived, supplemented by Auntie Ranie and her daughter Santi, came to the airport to bid him farewell. As they were driving to the airport, Sumi kept saying, "You better come home more often now. Perhaps next year."

"I don't know when I will be back. Perhaps I will come when I am ready to die," Kumaran had replied. The pall this created in the car was too much to bear, so he quickly said, "I was joking, of course. I will come next for Revati's wedding. Arrange one soon."